# Death *at the*
# Flea Circus

A NOVEL BY
*David Barker*

Bottle of Smoke Press

First Edition

ISBN-13:     978-1-937073-01-5 (paper)
             978-1-937073-00-8 (signed cloth)

Bottle of Smoke Press
902 Wilson Drive
Dover, DE 19904
www.bospress.net

For Judy,
who has always
been there for me

# CONTENTS

## Author's Note

As best I can tell, I wrote *Death at the Flea Circus* in the period 1968 to 1973. I was in college, an English major, my head full of the classics. I read the Romantic and French Symbolist poets, but also Sherlock Holmes stories, novels by Alain Robbe-Grillet and Richard Brautigan, and science-fiction stories. Judy and I were newlyweds, living near the sea in Long Beach, California. *Death at the Flea Circus* was not my first attempt at a novel, but it was the first novel that I felt was complete and worthy of publication.

While there is murder and uncertainty, the novel is not really a mystery, and the few violent scenes are cartoonish. I call it a surreal comic novel. There are time-travel elements, rendering the chronology as fluid as the overlapping identities of the narrators. I sought to create a unique story that would hold the reader's interest, keep him or her guessing as to where it was going next, with enough humor to offset the grim premise of a serial killer. I wanted to say something about the schizophrenic mood of the times, which began with Peace and Love, and ended with Altamont and Vietnam.

The story has its roots in a summer vacation I took with a high-school friend and his real-estate tycoon father, before I met my wife. We stayed at a hotel in Goleta, swam in the pool, and watched the sunbathing girls but were too shy to talk to them. Everything else in the book is the product of my imagination, fed by the literature I'd been exposed to in college, and bears no relationship to real people or events.

The novel went through four drafts. I still have a few chapters from the first draft, written in longhand, as well as second-draft chapters that I printed on a mimeograph machine and handed out in my writing class. The third draft exists as a complete typescript. With a few changes suggested by the Master of Arts committee, the fourth draft served as my thesis. The book as published is based on that fourth draft, with minor editing and corrections. Essentially, it's the novel I finished in January 1973.

Early on, I submitted the novel to major publishers in New York (they were not tempted) and then put it away and forgot about it for nearly 40 years. In late 2010, I sent a copy of the manuscript to Bill Roberts, asking him to keep it as backup in case the original was lost. To my delight, Bill liked the book and offered to publish it. He enlisted the aid of professional literary editor Christa Malone, who gently offered suggestions for ways the text could be improved. Thanks to Christa's invaluable editing and Bill's brilliant design work, this is the best possible edition of *Death at the Flea Circus*.

David Barker
April 2011

This book was written, in its entirety, shortly before I was born. In February 2008, David sent me eight chapters that he had self published in an extremely limited, photocopied edition for friends. I immediately sent him an e-mail letting him know that I loved what I had read and asked him to send me the full manuscript. In late 2010 he became concerned that there was only one physical copy of the manuscript (it had not yet been digitized) and he was worried that, without a backup, it was vulnerable to loss. The plan was for me to become a backup, of sorts, by having a full copy of all of his work in a second location. I received the manuscript and began reading it and immediately realized that it was even better than was hinted at by the eight-chapter excerpt that I had read three years earlier. At that point, I e-mailed David and asked for, and was granted, permission to publish this lost masterpiece.

Note that some of the words and spellings in this book are intentionally outdated. In typesetting the book, the decision was made to use the medial *s* (*f*) in titles only. Using this medial *s* in the text, although authentic to much of the book, would be difficult for modern readers to get used to and would pose a distraction.

*Death at the Flea Circus* is an amazing story that is difficult to classify. It's a hall of mirrors that's illusive and delusive, mysterious and fantastic. It's a wholly original package that's not neatly tied up with a bow. Once read, the book begs to be reread.

I am happy that this manuscript sat preserved for so long in an attic in Salem, Oregon, waiting for me to discover it and publish it as not only the first novel published by Bottle of Smoke Press but also the most involved production to date. I hope that it does not take another three years to receive and read the lost manuscripts of David's other novels, which include *Wraethrom, Hippies, Virgin Daughter,* and his current work in progress, *Stella Vero.*

Bill Roberts
April 2011

Death
at the
Flea Circus

# Chapter 1
## The Laſt Entry


Outside all is wetness and dark. Not black but a lack of visibility that makes the already thick and uncertain windows a cold, horrid grey. At my feet, wrapped in colored rags, is the blue fragile body of the 33$^{rd}$ whore. She has the smile of satisfaction on her dead lips. The crime is complete. I make a note in my inventory of the position of the body on the concrete floor and of some strange markings around the nipple of each breast. It is the last entry in my inventory. I leave by the back way to avoid the police and their bothersome talk.

It has been storming all night and the sea washes halfway up the street with each wave. I wade through the muddy seawater to where the sidewalk emerges from the tide, and up the street to the cathedral where they are holding midnight services. Inside is brightly lit. From the arched doorway of the transept, I can see the gleam of gold tiles in the mosaic encrusted walls. The priest sings in his purple robes.

# Chapter 2
## Excerpt from the Tranſcript of the Proceedings
## of the Inveſtigation into... Etc., Etc.

Authority: "When did you first meet her, Mister Barker?"

Barker: "Ah . . . I don't remember the date, the year. It was at a party, somebody's party."

A: "Yes, and what sort of a party was this?"

B: "What sort? Usual sort. I don't remember exactly what sort of a—"

A: "Did you—"

B: "I do remember however that someone brought some mushrooms, strange little mushrooms, and you lit one and smoked . . ."

A: "I did?"

B: "No, I meant we did."

A: "You and I?"

B: "No, those of us at the party."

A: "Well you said *I* . . ."

B: "No, I said *you*, meaning it in the abstract; you know, like *one*, or *they*, or *people*."

A: "Yes, I understand, much like the French *on*, *n'est-ce pas?*"

B: "Yes, quite."

A: "So people, or one, or they, lit this sliced mushroom and smoked it, is that correct?"

B: "Yes."

A: "What was the effect?"

B: "Narcotic."

A: "Then one might say it was a dope party, mightn't one?"

B: "Yes, one might say that."

A: "Yes, I suppose one might. But you don't remember the date of this party?"

B: "No."

A: "And did you smoke any of this drug, Mr. Barker?"

B: "Yes I did."

A: "And did the young lady?"

B: "I don't know. I don't think I met her until after that, much after . . . as I was leaving the party."

A: "All right. Tell us about this meeting, Mr. Barker."

B: "Well like I said, I was just leaving when I saw this young girl standing by the door. We decided to go for a walk. She told me her age and I kissed the back of her neck."

A: "Did you 'get it on' as they say?"

B: "No . . . I told her that in two years I'd marry her. She remained pure."

# Chapter 3
## Tools

They are pursuing. Tools. I must get tools. Nothing functions without proper care and maintenance; in this case it is already too late — I must be devious — repairs must be made. I do not believe that there is a piece of iron within twenty miles of this place; tools — probably none for a hundred miles. I remember my captor's voice; he lamented the loss of the cities.

The gulls are making some great fuss. They squawk and scatter light from the surface of the water. Perhaps it is over a fish, or some foul, tasteless organic matter floating on the backside of a wave's slope, dead for days. It may just be a scrap of white paper that caught their eye. The sun makes all things appear to grow.

The bolt on my pistol is jammed with rust, frozen with a dull, reddish-brown crust that seems to grow out of the crevice between the bolt and the tray in which it slides. It will not budge at all; the action is entirely frozen. With the proper tools, I may be able to make repairs. I scoff at my own necessity.

## Chapter 4
## A Note of an Entry to Be Made . . . Etc.


In my pocket is a marble, recovered from the earth at Long Beach, where I was digging in a friend's garden and discovered it among the roots and swollen, impotent bulbs. Its design is a gray swirl, with some parts clear and some parts opaque. I mean to make a note of it in my inventory of places and things.

misc.:

(The sand and water together on the bottom of my pants' legs makes the cuffs stiff, but it is the salt, I believe, that makes my skin taut over the bones and cartilage of my features.)

# Chapter 5
## A Paſſage

I had walked a full mile before I came to the spot where the cliffs jut up only five feet away from the foaming edge of the water, and the beach is narrowed to a sliver of sand. There is a wealthy person's house somewhere above, and the chain-link fence that forms the property boundary runs all the way down the slope of rock and onto this narrow spot in the beach, so that the space actually passable is only a foot or two wide unless you want to go out into the water. At high tide you would have to swim around. It suddenly occurs to me that this might be intended to keep people out of one side or the other. That is, one side might be private property, and this fence imposing itself onto the beach may be a sort of blockade or barrier. But I cannot imagine which side is which. If I cross, I may be trespassing. Yet, if I stay, I may be continuing to commit trespassage. The real crime, of course, is the act of entering through the pass. I cross through, and come upon a long stretch of beach blue with fog. Far off there is some sort of dark mass, like trees or figures, near the water's line. I approach with inevitable fear.

# Chapter 6
## Difcovery of the Corpfe of the 32$^{nd}$

I am making tea. The howl of the storm is terrible. My room is dark and cold, covered with the dust and dim light that is now everywhere. I have just returned from the Iron Works. My hunch was right; I found her behind the slag vat. She was mutilated. I used my handkerchief, the red and blue cowboy one, to cover her nudity. There was an amazing freshness to her skin, considering.

# Chapter 7
## The Dark Mafs at the End of the Beach

It is very far off, this dark mass on the edge of the surf. As I approach, it seems to recede. I'm puzzled, but a little relieved.

I've stopped to eat. It is something like noon. You can't see the sun, but its brightness is approximately overhead where twelve o'clock is in the sky. From out of the long pockets in my coveralls I take a small gray-green tin of food. Hardly food. A gritty, tasteless paste. The supply never diminishes, although I almost wish it would. Perhaps it grows in there, in the can, when the lid is on and it's dark inside, like a fungus. As I eat, I keep my eye on the black mass down the beach. I think now that maybe it's a group of tractors and trucks, and maybe a crane. There is something geometrical to the structure, but also vegetable. I ache for tools.

I walk and I walk and I walk and I walk and I walk and I walk and I am no closer to it.

# Chapter 8
## Another Excerpt from the Tranfcript of the
## Proceedings of the Inveſtigation Into . . .


Authority: "What exactly was your relationship with her?"

Barker: "As I said earlier, she remained pure. She was exceedingly beautiful, with white skin and golden hair. I believe she came out of the sea. She wore a small, perfect pearl as a necklace. It was on a gold chain, a very fine and delicate gold chain that looked as if the wind could snap it, and the pearl hung between her two breasts. They were full but small. She was a lovely girl. She had fine gold hairs around her vagina."

# Chapter 9
## An Air-Conditioned Cafeteria

The hum of the air blowers. A food smear at my elbow changes the light off the table. When someone last wiped this tabletop clean with a wet rag, the lines of water dried into a grain of reflection off the shiny surface. Grease goes against the grain. With my right thumb I change its directions. I obliterate it with my shirt sleeve, leaving only an area with a softer matte sheen than the rest of the top.

The air conditioning has a constant sound, like the pressure of water on the ears from underwater swimming. I picture a fat woman in her thirties, in a yellow bathing suit, blue lines crowding the back of her knees, and ripples of fat where enormous sections of flesh disappear into stiff bra cups. The pool throws green spots of light up that move across her chest. There is no sound at all, as if the ears are plugged with water from deep swimming. A wet rubbing of thighs. The dry heat of terry-cloth towels. Flashing hot cement. Then a splashing sound and screams.

The clinking of ice cubes in my glass. The light is very strange in here. Artificial light with its dark, metallic incandescence. I have my sunglasses on, which makes the chrome surfaces look transparent and unsubstantial, like highly polished dark metal. A throbbing vibration, like a distant earthquake, comes from somewhere and up through the table; it is probably a generator. A potted palm stands before the window. I can't see past the glass because of its smoked green tint. The plant is a dark rubber green. It is plastic, or else dead, poisoned by the cigarette butts in its sand.

Plunge. There is sudden and total silence. Only the inner sound of blood through the ears. A blind sweep down with arms thrown back in faith.

# Chapter 10
## Inventory

I made the notation of the gray-green marble in my inventory of places and things, and the blue ink turned brown with age in a matter of minutes. There is no set number of notations in my inventory; the objects, places, conditions, and events are merely absorbed into the whole body of the book, which is indeterminate in scope. There is no organizing principle. I have omitted nothing. This in itself makes me laugh, but the sound of my voice is destitute, as I am entirely alone here. A sample of entries:

— purple cabbage; 3 lrg. leaves.
— 2 old candles; organic-looking, maybe
  from the mayflower.
— sir walter raleigh's composure on the
  chopping block. admirable.
— kleenex from the goleta hotel.

# Chapter 11
## Laſt Remains of the 31ˢᵗ . . . Etc., &
## Mrs. Ghaſt Makes an Unuſual Offer

Upon receipt of a message containing valuable information from a certain unidentified source in the west side of the docks area, I immediately went to the home of a Mrs. Ghast, a comely young widow whom it has been my good fortune to employ over the years as a diviness. She was sitting by the gas furnace, reading Tennyson, when I came in. She immediately put on the tea, so that I might warm myself up on this cold and dreadful night while she read of things to come in the leaves. The message, "brass," meant nothing to her, but as soon as I heard it, I was ready to be off. She grabbed my arm as I moved to the door.

"Must you be off so soon?"

"I must."

"Wait just a short while," she said.

"What for?"

She kissed me full on the lips and then, unlacing the front of her blouse, put my hands up under her large warm tits. They burned like little fried fishes. She pulled me down on top of her on the parlour davenport and clawed at the lump between my legs.

"I must be off," I said. "Life or death."

"Come back later tonight." She sat upright with her breasts and stomach bare.

"I shall."

"Promise?"

"Absolutely."

I got a cab to take me to the Blue Hogg Inn, and it was there, in a bathtub in a dingy little room on the third floor, that I found the body. The lithe little thing looked as if she weighed no more than a hundred pounds. Her clothes were torn and she had poppies in her hair. It was a messy job. Her cheeks were still rose tinged and her throat was flushed. The rain was coming down miserably hard. I sat for a while on the wooden stairs leading up to the room and had a cigarette.

# Chapter 12
## Narrative from the Tranſcript of the Proceedings of the Inveſtigation into Several . . . Etc., Etc.

Authority: "And what exaĉtly were the circumstances surrounding consummation of the 'affair'?"

Barker: "Ah . . . that's difficult. I don't aĉtually remember the first . . . like I said—she remained pure . . . the foam . . . Greek I believe it is, or is it Latin? Yet I recall the next, the second, instance quite clearly. . . ."

A: "Where were you?"

B: "There were no street names."

A: "The time?"

B: "Night. We slept. She awoke screaming . . . at nothing at all. People were moving about outside . . . but I don't believe they paid us any regard. Screams as though something hung over her. She could not sleep and we decided to try it again. Too many people about to pull it off, though. We got in the car and drove out to where the lights ended. I wanted to stop here among the straggly brush, but she said a better place was just a bit further out. We got out of the car and, after crossing a dry, rocky gulch, came to a stony ridge that led into the deep woods. At the end of the ridge, she said, was a cave where we could do it without distraĉtion. She went ahead, and I followed. There were snakes all about—banded constriĉtors. Yellow and black, and some nearly ten feet long. I wondered that they didn't strike at us, until she showed me that they were dead, only dried-out shells of skin that crumbled when you stepped on them. I was still cautious, however. I was a little angered that she took their harmlessness for granted. And it was a good thing too, because one moved for my leg as I made my way around it, and it only stopped when I crushed its skull with a large stone. I felt very uncomfortable. I could still hear the people towards the lights. But the cave was very dark and silent. So that touch seemed more intense. She immediately gushed when I rubbed her there. She was wild and it was all I could do to wait out my time."

A: "What did you think as this happened?"

B: "I thought of the lighting of torches, and of the dust upon our car as it sat parked off the road in the brush."

# Chapter 13
## The Catholic Agent Receives His Fee

I went back to my room on the shore, where the sea washes halfway up the city streets, lit the kerosene lamp with a sulphurous match, brushed the dust and cob from the accompt book (you know the one: *Abstract of the Accompt of Payments Made . . .* etc., done up in black morocco by the so-called Naval Binder), and marked receipt of my fees in the Blue Hogg Affair. Pounds, shillings, pence. Strange business this.

Although it was very late when I returned, Mrs. Ghast was still sitting up, in her night dress, the dark wind howling bestially outside, she stitching and listening to the overseas broadcast, which came in quite clearly considering the weather. We heard a drinking report from Sydney, and sheep reports from New Zealand. With my penknife I made some repairs in the brasswork about the quarters and, while at the window, happened to notice that a thick fog was rolling in. We felt quite alone in the world, wrapped for sleep in our private grey cloud bank. Mrs. Ghast's breasts were pink and swollen with sleep. We gave it a rub for a while, but she was beyond the hour of arousement. Strange business this.

We retired to her cozy bed and Mrs. Ghast soon dropped off, but I could not sleep. As badly in need of rest as I was, my mind was on the gruesome events of the past 24 hours, and whenever I would begin to drift off into oblivious slumber, some horrid image of a young girl's corpse would fright me into consciousness. Several times I sat up with a startled scream, but the scream was in my nightmares, and hadn't actually issued from my lips, so that fortunately Mrs. Ghast wasn't unnecessarily awakened. I was desirous that she remain ignorant of the tormented obsession in which this series of crimes held me. I gained only a few minutes' sleep total, and had eaten naught except tea and a pastry all day, so bewildered and horrified was I by my ghastly discoveries. Always too late—the fiend was one step ahead of me. The slayings were linked by one common element: invariably, the victims looked more in a state of pleasure than pain. In all a flush over the entire face and extending down the breasts to the thighs and private parts. The nipples erect and lubrication of the private tract. In all the same puzzling smile. All gaily clad or decorous in some manner. I was suddenly struck with the compulsion to be out in the fog where I could ponder the case more clearly and perchance gain fresh evidences. I arose, dressed, donned my deerstalker, and left Mrs. Ghast behind quietly locked doors. Knowing my ways, she would not be too disturbed to find me gone.

The fog was marvelous; holding the glow of the gas lamps, it created a luminous blindness more haunting than mere darkness. I decided to walk along Dram, an unusual street, of importance only to persons of the night in that its shops and cafes, unlike any others in the city, were open all night, and in fact only at night, the general hours of business for the street being 10 at night to 3 in the morning. Quite a chill was out, and I hastened my step so as to arrive as soon as possible at Wimpole's, a midnight second-hand clothing store specializing in bargains in the way of fine used clothing of the last century. I knew from experience that the best buys were on the sidewalk racks, and in no time at all I found what I was looking for: a heavy, gray-tweed combination overcoat and hooded cape, which, with several secret inside pockets and a red silk lining like new, was a steal at 5 pounds. The merchant, a somnambulist with pale blue eyes, gave me a queer look as he took my gold, and pointed out to me the luxurious sable lining in the collar, with which I was doubly convinced of my good buy.

My next stop was at Van Woo Fong's, where I bought an ounce of Latakia, as I was in need of a smoke, and a little trinket on which I had had my eye for several months. It was a 16th century silver alchemist's powder box, about an inch deep and 3 inches in diameter, which I thought might serve well as a matchbox. The lid was a collapsible sundial, with some rather quaint Coptic markings, and the bottom had an enameled portrait of some Byzantine saint in the manner of the mosaics at Ravenna. Just the sort of thing to come in handy when one least expects. I was now prepared to walk the fog with my pipe and new coat to warm me.

I continued up Dram, brushing past the drunken sailors, linseed oil women, past the whores who lingered in the dark of cobblestone alleyways and who cooed from mossy walls in the Gothic grottos under bridges and by the aqueduct, past the blue-eyed children selling rotten fish from buckets of cold, murky water alongside the cafes, and past the ghoulish young students who pawed over old tomes in the dusty midnight bookstalls, all the while methodically puffing at my pipe and meditating upon the crimes.

At the top of the hill, where Dram ends, I turned from its well-lit walk to the broken, muddy streets of Crux, a wide road, more alley than street, lined on both sides with sheet-tin warehouses. It was much darker along here, and quieter, the only sounds at all being the dripping of moisture from rusted pipes onto the pavement and the feet of rats along the stone.

Strange business this. If only word would arrive from Madrid.

# Chapter 14
## The Bombed Apartment

It got colder as the sun went down. The foamy surf turned from white to blue, and the dark mass down the way grew indistinct and then I could no longer see it at all. I sat down, shivering, in the sand and tried to unjam my pistol once more before leaving the relative safety of the beach. It was getting much too cold to stay, and a chilling wind picked up off the ocean, blowing the hair in my eyes as I tried to break the rust free from the bolt. It was impossible without tools.

When I scaled the hill and walked far enough inland, I discovered that the destruction was more widespread than I had thought. What had been a large housing complex stretching for nearly a half mile had been almost entirely reduced to rubble: twisted wire in puzzled, pockmarked slabs of concrete and stucco. More of the same could be seen in both directions along the coast and inland. But the growing dimness soon hid all that. There were a few two-story apartments still partly standing, and I decided these would be the best I would find for the night. I climbed the stairs to enter one, thinking only of the tools I needed to fix the gun. It never occurred to me to be on my guard here. When I entered the room I was startled to see two Korean children, nearly infants, sitting on top of a large wooden chest. No, there were no children. I cannot stand their faces dull with shock nor their pale dirty cheeks nor bloodied eyes. The chest alone remains. It contains the entire worldly possessions of the Korean family: old willow china, silverware, ravels of fine linen and silks. I believe the parents were murdered, shot in the head and left lying in the corner. The children still guard the chest. No, there are no children.

From the window a thousand stars can be seen, like bright, eternal all-night laundromats. I lie in bed, listening to the rock-and-roll station play, and make notations in my inventory, while dreaming of the white thighs of the whores on Signal Hill, beyond the turnoff from the steep, unlit wind off the narrow road.

# Chapter 15
## In the Pool

I am lingering in the shadowy blue water in the northern corner of the deep end of the Goleta Hotel swimming pool. Although it is shadowy, the water is not really blue. It is the tiles beneath that are blue. This is done by pool manufacturers to make the water look more inviting; this is very much like the beads of moisture on the glass in a Coke ad. I am resting with my back to the pool's edge, with my hands in the gutter that runs around the pool, and I'm letting my legs float up to just beneath the surface. This is quite relaxing, although there is a slight tension in the shoulders because of the crucifixion-like pose. I rest back my head on the gutter ledge and think of being in the air-conditioned cafeteria, while deeply inhaling the chlorine-smelling air. My hair is wet, the water dripping from it down both cheeks, along the corners of my mouth, and down either side of my chin where it drips off into the pool.

The sun is very high, just off to one side, and I am in the shade of a palm tree. The pool is in a courtyard enclosed on four sides by first and second story rooms. Above, at the far end from me, a middle-aged woman is standing at the balcony rail, turning her left eye into the sun, while the shade from her straw hat covers the right. She is wearing sunglasses, has a white straw purse hooked over her right arm, and is playing with a key ring in her left hand. She has most of her weight on her left foot, and the right leg has a slight bend at the knee. She turns towards my direction and squints as both eyes are now in the sun. She readjusts her hat to shade them.

I am thinking once again of the cafeteria. It is almost closing time and the waitress is wiping the coffee rings from the Formica-topped tables. She pulls with her a cart into which she places the dirty dishes, spoons, and paper trash. There is a can into which she scrapes the uneaten food with a white rubber spatula. The fans are humming monotonously.

# Chapter 16
## Parakeets

I've decided to stay here awhile. At least until the peak of summer when it's warm enough to sleep on the beach at night. I've cleaned the place up somewhat, but don't know what to do with the chest. The children don't bother me. They sing all day like parakeets. I spend afternoons gathering seed for them. They are beginning to have a lovely yellow plumage. Foreigners are unpredictable.

Every morning I walk down to the beach to take a look at the dark mass. I still can't make it out, although every day it seems a bit closer. It is either moving slowly in this direction, or else it's growing. The rest of the day I spend looking for tools in the rubble. I never have visitors.

# Chapter 17
## Mrs. Ghaſt Makes Do

Awaking alone, Mrs. Ghast began to pout. The tears rolled down her cheeks as she sat up in bed wearing only a thin nightgown. "Where the fuck's he off to?" she muttered. She grabbed a candle from the nightstand, lay back, spread her legs apart, and made do.

# Chapter 18
## Inftance of the 30<sup>th</sup>

The spell of Dram Street, with all its curious charms, soon wore off as I slowly stalked Crux. The place had an unwholesome emptiness to it, and I began wishing that I were safe back in Mrs. Ghast's room, feeling her up on the davenport and drinking hot chocolate from a Chinatown mug.

Ahead, lying under one of the few street lamps along Crux, was a young girl whom I recognized from the pool at the Goleta Hotel. I took out my inventory and marked "30<sup>th</sup>." She wore a long calico dress. Her head rested in a pool of dark blood, and she had a countenance of perfect peace. I must have stood there staring at her for five minutes. Then the policeman's whistle and clatter of boots on the pavement, and I dashed into the Glass Works.

# Chapter 19
## The Bus Arrives

Thirty-three wayward girls from somewhere in the Midwest arrived by bus at the Goleta Hotel. I was in the pool at the time doing surface dives. It was Paul who told me about it; he had just returned from his daily mile jog and had seen the bus pull up into the parking lot. The girls stayed seated while the driver and two women counselors went into the manager's office to talk business. Paul had come directly to tell me; he was still in his cut-off jeans and T-shirt, sweating profusely but not panting too hard, and holding the 2 dollar pocket watch by which he timed his runs. It was to keep his lungs in shape for playing the trumpet. He ran daily after an hour's series of exercises and scales. I would sit in the hotel room with him and the metronome, reading while he made short bursts of ascending and descending notes, and then he would run while I swam. The pool was usually empty at this hour. Paul's father was out almost every day on real-estate business.

# Chapter 20
## Madrid

I sit in my room, which is dark with the dark that is everywhere now, and watch a spider build her nest across my window. Soon the window glass is covered with gauze. She moves over to my bookcase and begins work on it. This can only mean one thing.

I go to the home of a prominent archæologist and close friend, Sir Richard Wrought. I am admitted to a stylish waiting room by a servant. There are two full-length mirrors in large gilt frames on opposite walls that reflect one into the other as in a barber shop. In the pit of each is a dark greenish mass where mirrors and multiples of my own image dissolve into the opaqueness of the glass.

I am shown into Sir Richard's magnificent library, with its depository of thousands of volumes, its glass cases containing Sir Richard's world-renowned collection of minute bird bones in its entirety, and its display of over 300 marble busts of famous men that line the walls and fill the few unoccupied spaces in the bookshelves. I am quite familiar with the room, as Sir Richard allows me free access to his library so as to aid me in my studies and researches. This he does in both the professional spirit and as an act of friendship.

Sir Richard's teenage daughter enters the room from somewhere amongst the mountains of books. We have met a few times already.

"Is Sir Richard in?" I ask. "It's urgent."

"No, but come with me," she answers mysteriously. We exit through a passageway between two enormous stacks of scientific works, and I follow her up a dark stairway.

"Where is he, if I may ask?"

"You certainly may. He's in Madrid."

"Madrid?"

We enter at the top of the stairs into a small (considering the size of the mansion) but extremely comfortable room with a large, luxuriously covered bed and a small single lamp burning on a bedstand beside it.

"Yes, Madrid, digging," she answers.

"Oh." She unzips her dress and steps out of it. She has a slender, luscious figure. "How quaint of Sir Richard," I mumble, sticking a cigarette between my lips and lighting it.

She unties her hair and lets it fall down upon her smooth white back and small, adolescent breasts. She flops back on the bed with her legs spread apart and gives a sigh. "Yes," she says, "I suppose it is rather quaint of Daddy."

I can't keep my eyes off the little patch of freshly sprouted hair.

# Chapter 21
## Excerpt from the Tranſcript of Tape Recordings Made During the Interview with Mr. Barker Conducted as a Neceſſary Inveſtigation into Certain Sundry Affairs as Relating to Etc., Etc.

Authority: "And what was the cause of all this?"

Barker: "Cause? I don't believe there was any such thing as might be called a cause. . . ."

A: "I mean, perhaps, what exactly brought all this about? What was it that in the first place—"

B: "Oh, well that all depends on what you mean by *first*. In the *first place*, of course, there was nothing. We have no terms for those sorts of things. But in the *first place*, well that's another matter."

A: "Yes! Do you . . . [this section of the tape has been mysteriously mutilated] . . . which of course we could all understand."

B: "Yes, I think that's it."

A: "And where did this take place?"

B: "Ah, it . . . Is the microphone on?"

A: "Yes the micro—"

B: "Somebody's fucking with it. Who's? . . . Somebody's trying—"

A: "—ter Barker! The microphone is . . . you please sit down and contin—!"

B: "Somebody's . . . the fucking microph– . . . another word until the—"

A: "—don't sit down immediately and stop using that—call the guard! No one is . . . -crophone!"

B: (Blowing into microphone) "Yes, it's on now. Yes, I think it's on now."

A: "It was on all the time, Mr. Barker."

B: "Like hell it was."

A: "Please try to calm down, Mr.—"

B: "Like hell it was."

A: "You can in no way harm or offend me by using that tone."

B: "Awww."

A: "Do you want to continue?"

B: "Continue what?"

A: "The questioning."

B: "As if I had a choice."

A: "Yes, as if you had a choice."

B: "All right, sure, of course, why not?"

A: "Thank you, Mr. Barker. And where were we? . . . ah yes. And where did this take place?"

B: "Ah, what were we talking about? Oh yes, I remember, ah, where did this take place, ah, it was in Long Beach, behind a grocery store."

A: "Do you remember the name of the store?"

B: "Foodarama, something like that, yeah it was Foodarama."

A: "And where was this store, the 'Foodarama,' located?"

B: "It was in Long Beach. Do you want me to draw you a map?"

A: "Yes, that might be nice. I'm quite fond of maps."

(Sound of Mr. Barker's pencil scratching against the paper.)

A: "Ah, what street's that?"

B: "Oh, that's Pine, that's Pine Street, and this one's Long Beach Boulevard."

A: "Yes, I see. So this way is north, right?"

B: "No no, that's east. This way is north."

A: "And so the ocean would be out here, right?"

B: "Yeah, here, I'll draw in the waves."

A: "Why don't you add a couple fish."

B: "Think I ought to?"

A: "Sure, don't be timid."

B: "It's not timidity."

A: "Well, what is it then?"

B: "Well, they'd be terribly out of scale."

A: "So?"

B: "Well, this is an official map and all that, isn't it?"

A: "Yes, I suppose you're right; it might be considered foolish of us."

B: "Foolish of you. It doesn't much matter if I look foolish to them or not, does it?"

A: "Yes, you're right. Foolish of me."

B: "Well, I could put in a couple of oil rigs."

A: "Would they be in scale?"

B: "Close enough. No one's going to make a fuss."

# Chapter 22
## The Sea Gives Forth

This morning, while walking along the beach about 50 yards from the apartment, I found a bottle that had apparently washed ashore in the high night tides. There was something inside, but the sand and ocean residue was so heavily encrusted on the bottle that I couldn't tell what it was through the glass. I sat down on a large flat rock that lay at the base of the cliff and tried to unscrew the cap. It was tight with rust. The thought that a note might be inside thrilled me to no end. I scraped some of the crap off the side on the sharp edge of the rock until I could see a little inside. It was definitely paper, and I thought I could just make out a faint scrawl of ink that might be a word. And that word might be part of a sentence. It might prove to be a whole note. I was thrilled. Then I had a terrible thought: a small amount of sea water had somehow leaked into the bottle. If the ink wasn't permanent then perhaps the water had washed off enough of the ink to make my note illegible. Tossing and turning with the waves, every part of the note would surely be soaked. I prayed that the ink was permanent. I gritted my teeth and smashed the bottle against the rock. The note was limp and salty and smelled foul. I let it dry for a hour or so in the sun until it was strong enough not to tear as I held it in my hands and read it. I hadn't done any laundry in a long time and this brought back fond memories. I sat with the note flat and limp beside me on the rock, and day-dreamed of the free-dry-with-every-wash laundromats back home in Long Beach. As I said, in an hour it was dry enough to handle. It read (in a moronic scrawl):

Dear Lad,
Having a wonderful time. Wish you were here. Have found many good bones. Re: your inquiry; sorry but no information yet—Will send you word as soon as able. Love to my little girl & keep up the spirit,
Cordially,
Sir Rich[rd] Wrought
Apr. 1st, 1786
Our Lady of Luxury Hotel
Madrid.

When I returned to the apartment, I found the parakeets lying dead on the bottom of their cage. I stood in silence considering this when two old men from the Salvation Army came to the door, saying that they had orders to haul the chest away.

Authority: "What was the situation at this time?"
Barker: "Pain . . . absolute pain . . . and dejeƈtion. She
was radiant, and I was no more than a slug. I gave up
all hopes of possession. It's amazing how we can go
on that way. The rain was always outside, dribbling
sadly and sorely down the panes. In some ways it
hurt more, but in others it soothed me. I looked
forward to it; it was a sort of release. I relished it, the
pain and the melancholy weather, to be truthful, as it
was all I had left of dignity and beauty. I began not
to really mind after a while, although it still hurt me
to the quick. We got to be so damned fucking grown
up about it, so mature, to go on like that in a
friendly, even intimate way. I used to sit afternoons
over a cup of coffee in the cafeteria, just hoping she
might come by. All my afternoons were sad and
worn like that. Sometimes she would . . . and then
what? The glistening pain in the eyes—beauty! Such
horrid beauty! . . . It was almost ugly . . . the sadness,
uncontrollable weeping, and the wetness of green
all around. I remember watching the clouds gather; I
would often stand in the cold wind, shivering, for
there was no one to tell me not to."

# Chapter 24
## In the Pool

My shoulders are getting cold in the air so I decide to swim a little more. I dunk my whole body beneath the water, push off from the side of the pool with the fleshy pad under my toes, and shoot out into the water like a slow-motion projectile; my arms are extended before me and my legs are straight. I keep my knees unbent. The only kick I use is a slight paddling of the feet, bending only at the ankles. By this method I can travel three-fourths the length of the pool without stroking my arms or kicking my legs. I go the remaining fourth by maintaining my momentum with a single frog-like stroke of my arms, bringing them flat against my sides, and at the same time executing a single scissor thrust of my legs. I glide along silently under the water with my head tilted up so that I can see when I have reached the other side. As soon as I surface I can once again hear the poolside noises: the gurgling of water in the gutters, the wind in the dry, sheath-like leaves of the palm, and weak, static music from a transistor radio.

I am no longer alone out here. The radio belongs to a young girl of about 15 who is lying back on a canvas and wood folding lounge chair. She has a bathing suit on, a bright orange bikini that contrasts strikingly with the deep brown tan of her slender body, and facedown a paperback book is laid spread open in her lap. Her delicate gold hands with long pink nails rest on the glossy covers of the book, and her eyes are closed. One strap of the bathing suit top has fallen from her shoulder, and there is a soft white line where she didn't tan. The little wisps of hair in her bangs brush with the wind against her forehead and, on the sides where it is longer, across her cheeks and the bridge of her nose. She seems to be sleeping. I hadn't noticed her coming; she just appeared as I was underwater. She's one of those from the Home, but seems entirely decent, just lying there asleep.

# Chapter 25
# The Dark Maſs

Every day now I walk a little farther down the beach towards the dark mass before turning around and heading back home towards the bombed-out apartment. There is no reason for me to return early anymore now that the children are gone. The days are getting longer, so that by the time the sun sets each day, I have gone a little farther and have come a little closer to the dark mass. Yet, I am still unable to make out what it is. I know, however, that it will become my whole life. There seems to be an activity around it, a radiance, like many brightly colored bathers in the glare of the sea. It may, however, only be the liquid distortion of heat waves off the sand. Perhaps I will know by this time next year.

I am sitting at a corner table in the cafeteria. They have turned the air conditioning off, as it began to rain a half hour or so ago, and the dining room has filled with students seeking refuge from the weather. There is a constant clamor of amazement at the rain, and the swishing, vinyl sound of collapsed umbrellas. Hot food smells from the steam table. The clatter of heavy white restaurant stoneware. The rich perfume that hangs in vapors about the collars of brown-haired girls. Out in the rain, down the walls and by the stone and brick sides of classrooms, the half-gray dark waits. From a blue fountain pen I draw cryptograms and acrostics, anagrams and Coptics, mazes, epigrams, segmentum and rubrics. Da Vinci orders a cheeseburger "heavy on the onions." Under his coat, protected from the rain, I spy the vellum boards of his notebook.

# Chapter 27
## Longman, Hurſt, Rees, Orme & Brown

I sat in Mrs. Ghast's parlour, reading a little book I had picked up in Dram Street on my way home from the university, entitled *An Inquiry into the History of Anglo-Saxon Pathos from Beowulf and Other Classicks to the Rolling Stones,* anonymous, "a newly enlarged and greatly improved edition," London: Printed for Longman, Hurst, Rees, Orme & Brown, Paternoster-Row, 1805, when I chanced to look up and see in the window a familiar and grotesque face. It was the street beggar I had encountered on Crux, who had followed me the duration of that street and for half of Dram. He smiled toothlessly and held up a greasy fish, mouthing the words, "You want to buy?" then rubbed his thumb against his forefingers to indicate coin.

"No," I said, "I don't want to buy. Definitely not."

He held up a different fish, larger, even more greasy looking, and obviously half rotten. He smiled idiotically and mouthed the words again.

"No! I don't want to buy!"

"You buy!" he mouthed, his smile turning to an evil sneer.

I went over to the window, pulled down the shade, and tried to continue reading.

# Chapter 28
## Penance

Old dustmen, hating the opera, put out the lamp lights along Dram Street one by one. (Three-fourths of the world is in darkness. Yet the gutters are beginning to fill with gold.) They shuffle with their snuffers, coughing and extinguishing, blind with soot, and, when asked, reveal only their name, route number, and penitential sentence.

I stalk behind them in the fog, whistling and twirling my cane, waiting for the end.

Someone tells me of a good English mystery on TV and I hurry home to catch it. I miss the end.

# Chapter 29
## In the Pool

Turning away from the sleeping girl, I spit out my last bit of breath to clear the water from my mouth and then draw in a fresh breath. I brush the hair from my eyes and take a small surface dive which brings me right to the bottom, so that my chest scrapes against the gritty floor of the pool. I can reach the bottom by only a surface dive at this, the shallow end, whereas in the deep end, the twelve-foot, a crouched dive from the pool's edge would be necessary in order to reach bottom.

Using a frog stroke, I explore the floor, my eyes wide open as the little bubbles of air escaping from my nostrils brush up against my cheeks. I see something circular and almost transparent as the light from the surface casts its shadow on the bottom, diffusing it and doubling the penumbras of its image. I sweep at it with my hand and it turns out to be only a hair curled in a loop. I thought it might be a lens or a plastic fruit juice bottle cap or some other solid but transparent object. Light traveling through water is very deceptive like that.

# Chapter 30
## Fifh

I had gotten back to my reading for a few
minutes when a buzz came at Mrs. Ghast's front door.
At first I was furious, thinking that it was the street
beggar again with his rotten fish, but it turned out to be
a special-delivery postman. I signed for the letter,
dropping a large silver coin into his blue and gold cap by
way of a tip. It was obviously from Sir Richard; I was
excited: long awaited information from Madrid! With
haste I tore the envelope to shreds and unfolded the
letter:

Dear Lad,
Sorry, but this is not the "word from Madrid"
for which you have been waiting so eagerly,
but merely an old man's necessary and pathetic
reaching out for the hand of a friend in times
of trouble. That is to say, I am not writing
because I am now able to help you in the
matter of the 33 wayward girls (which I am yet
unable to do, despite the fact that I am very
willing), but rather, because I petition you for
help in a small matter that has arisen here at
the hotel recently. To get to the heart of the
matter, we (the excavating party and I: noble
doctors Smithe, Jones, Applebaum, Casey &
Hernandez) have gotten into a slight row with
the management, who claim that one of the
members of our party stole into the hotel
basement midnight last and vandalized the
ancestral tomb. The hotel management is of one
family, and has been such for centuries, the
Gonadez family. The patriarch of this noble
band of Castilian hooligans, Sr. Guadaloupe
Joseff Manuel etc. etc. Gonadez, a gentleman of

103 years, descended into the basement midnight last in order to pay his respects to the
family dead, as he does every midnight (except
in leap years, when he goes down at noon), when
he found the family altar containing the
family relics (the fossil tooth of the family
founder, a Cro-Magnon landlord who raised
bulls for the ring, & the petrified teat of his
wife) totally destroyed, and the family graves
themselves violated. I inspected the site
myself, and indeed, the bones of that ancient
and ignorant family are gone. I tried to
explain that we had no use for the bones of
his family, and that the deed must have been
perpetrated by some common ghoul or grave
robber, but he would not hear of it. He insists
that, because we are archaeologists, well
versed in both digging and bones, that we are
therefore logically guilty. He threatens to go
to the police, unless we come across with a
cash settlement immediately, to the tune of
20,000 pesetas in small gold coins. I do not
relish rotting for fifteen or twenty years in
a Spanish jail, so I am asking of you a favor:
go to my daughter and tell her that you have
my instructions to sell the Rembrandt. She
will give it to you, and will you please take
it to a Mr. Gruntlehawk of 113 Dram Street, an
antiquarian and fine art dealer who has
offered me 1 1/2 million for it on several
occasions. Ask for $850,000 immediate cash, and
he's sure to buy. Send me the $800,000, give my
daughter $40,000 for living expenses, and keep
the extra 10 thousand for yourself as a fee in
this matter. Hurry!

> yours cordially,
> Sir Rich<sup>rd</sup> Wrought
> Our Lady of Luxury Hotel
> Madrid, Aug. 19, 1914

# Chapter 31
## Perufing on Dram

Upon receipt of the $40,000 deriving from the sale of her father's Rembrandt, Sir Richard Wrought's daughter went immediately to the Great Western Bookshop, a hole-in-the-wall establishment on Upper Dram housed between the Max Ernst Memorial College of Frottage and the New Irish Politics Center. The shop was a converted shoe-shine stand, and there still remained black boot stains on the shelves. Books purchased from the shop gave off a sinister smell of polish and sweat.

After browsing, comparing, picking and choosing, Sir Richard's daughter decided on five books for purchase:

*Famous American Vegetables: Their Thoughts and Deeds,* by Almone P. Horticle, Master of Botanical Arts at Harvard School of Science. A fat, shabby volume published at Boston in the year 1873. With 28 designs on wood by eminent artists. Faded purple binder's cloth, spine broken. $4.50.

*Picture Dictionary of the Love Arts.* Anonymous. Privately printed. Circa 1920. Large folio with full page photographic plates in sepia tone. In vellum. Well thumbed but good condition. $20.

*Death at the Flea Circus: A Maledictorian Address on the Atrocities of Youth, Being the Tale of a Psychotic Adolescent Poet and the Spiritual Crisis He Encounters One Summer at a Desolate Seaside Resort for Unemployed Lizards.* Bound in white buckram. J. M. Dent & Sons, London, 1927. $1.25.

*So Who'll Eat This Year?: A Series of Essays on the Birthday Cake Ritual in America & Its Relation to the Darker Side of Human Nature.* Edited by Kirk Clammon Whit. Contributions by Salmon P. Chase, James Anthony Springer, Miss Olivia Parks, Horace and Nathan Brant, James Montgomery, Wallace Beery, Edsel Ford & many others; With Special Introduction by "Sheriff" John. 12 Color Plates illustrating the History of Birthday Cake Decoration. In green speckled paper. $.75

*Fiat Lux, or Let There Be Light; The Complete Electrician's Manual,* by Saint Thomas of Elderberry. Lyons, 1553. In whole contemporary calf binding by John of Cork. Gilt back, boards. "Collated & Perfect by Sir R. W$^{rt}$, 1833," Rare wide margin copy. $500.

The shop owner, a bald little fellow with black-stained fingers, wrapped up the books in brown sack paper and tied the parcel with kite string. Sir Richard's daughter made out a check for 527 dollars and 50 cents, and received a dollar's change so that she could buy two packs of cigarettes on the way home. She would hide them in the hollow bust of Calvin. Her mother and the maids would never find them there.

# Chapter 32
## In the Pool

I had drifted now to the eastern corner of the pool when a shiny metallic disk caught my eye about five feet off. It was too far away to be seen clearly, but appeared to be made of chrome and resting on the bottom. When I got to it, I found that it was some sort of drainage plug and that it was firmly anchored to the bottom. I was looking for something substantial to bring up with me. On what little breath I had left, I swam a zigzag towards the center of the pool, into about eight-foot water where I saw something small and dark on the bottom, slowly rolling towards the deeper end. I surfaced, exhaled, and drew my breath in a hurry so that the moving object wouldn't escape me, and dove below, a little to the north, the direction in which it moved. At first I didn't see it. When I did, I saw that it had come upon a steeper slope, and was rolling rapidly into the deep end. The water in the deep end was darker, and I soon lost sight of it as the darkness made it indistinct and the growing distance completely obliterated it.

# Chapter 33
## On the Beach

One of the Korean children has returned. He is whimpering about his dead parakeet. I tell him that his parakeet has gone far away and will never come back. *Where is he now?* He's in parakeet heaven, I suppose. *Is he happy there?* Yes, he's happy. The child wanders off down the beach (in the direction of the dark mass) and I never see him again.

I took a coach out to the Blue Hogg Inn late Thursday evening in order to investigate certain undisclosed leads, clues that haven't been brought before the attention of the police, and was in the garden taking soil samples and pacing off the distance from the gas meter to the roadway, when the fellow who keeps bar in the lobby came out to tell me that three armed messengers had just arrived in front on bicycles saying that they had a special delivery letter for me. My heart leaped thinking that it might be *the news* from Madrid.

Dear Lad,

Sorry, but no news yet re: you-know-what. Just wrote to say I received the monies and am grateful to you for helping me out of this scrape. The kindly old Signor, Mr. Gonadez, has dropped all his previous charges against our party, and we are free once more to move with Liberty to and from our excavation site, or as we affectionately call it, "The Pit." All this, of course, only after the payoff. Have found many good bird bones. So sorry to hear about the death of your Goldfinch—assassins, you say? Nasty business all around. Love to my little girl,

in fealty yours,
Sir Richaurd Wrogtt
Our Blessed Lady of
Loyalty Hotel, Madrid
Easter Mass, 1463

# Chapter 35
## Mrs. Ghaſt Reads the Morning Paper

"Here's an odd article," said Mrs. Ghast as we sat at the breakfast table sipping our coffee. She spread the paper out flat in front of her and read aloud the following:

(GOLETA) Aug. 6th. Sea creature invades land after plaguing beach residents. The Goleta Gazetteer Independent Liberty Sun News Agency interviewed Police Chief Beetlebaulm about rumors of a sea serpent Wednesday night at a specially called secret press conference held in the basement of the Goleta Chocolate Factory. According to Chief Beetle-baulm, residents of Goleta Shores Apartment Complex (the only buildings left standing after the 1965 Hydrogen Bomb Test conducted on Carpinteria Beach in which 45,382 transient lemon-pickers were accidentally killed) have for the past few months reported a strange phenome-non on the beach, visible only from the water's edge. Although 513 reports of a U.C.O. (Unidenti-fied Coastal Object) were received, police failed to investigate because, in Chief Beetlebaulm's words, "a bunch a' looney cranks live on the beach." Police files contain hundreds of citizen reports of a "strange dark mass at the end of the beach." Some descriptions offered by eyewitnesses claim that the object appears at times to recede and at times to come closer, while others claim that the object grows and shrinks, in "an eerie, fungusoid pulsa-tion." One eyewitness, Ed Hanks, an 82-year-old retired shoe salesman interviewed by the Goleta Gazetteer Independent Liberty Sun News Agency, described the phenomenon in these terms: "It's the darnedest thing I ever saw all of my 80-odd years. Looked as if some blamed fool had tried to erase the sky with a dirty eraser and left a dirty smudge."

Rumor turned to panic Monday night when a Goleta family of five who were picnicking on the beach watched in shocked amazement as the "blob" moved up off the beach and inland, towards the town of Goleta. According to Chief Beetlebaulm, a "slimy black trail about twenty feet wide" was left by the creature as it crossed Highway One. The police are optimistic that the object has bypassed Goleta, as "there is nothing here that he could want," but local residents are not so optimistic. Harvey's Firearms reports an 800% increase in gun sales.

I had been listening very intently to what Mrs. Ghast was reading. This was a factor in the case I hadn't counted on.

"Well," she said, staring up at me from the paper, "what do you think?"

I got up and began pacing the floor. "Tell me, Mrs. Ghast, what do the stars tell you of this?"

She quietly got up and walked over to the cabinet where she took out a black cloth and a highly polished quartz crystal ball. She returned to the table, spread out the black cloth, sat down, placed the ball in the center of the cloth, and went into a reverie. A thin, spiritual voice came out of her throat; her eyes were blank.

"According to Jupiter, the City of Goleta is a very high magnetic field for the month of August. Saturn says the element in question may be a huge mass of iron filings attracted by the unusually high magnetic forces in the area. The center of the field is slowly shifting from the sea's edge to downtown Goleta. . . ."

# Chapter 36
## On the Beach

Chaos this morning. The dark mass is gone. I think It's been scared away by the hundreds of persons who have recently swarmed to the beach in order to catch a glimpse of It. I can hardly blame the poor thing. I don't know what I'll do with my mornings now, I've become so accustomed to walking down the beach to get a better look at It every day. I was making good progress. Now all that is over. Unless It returns. Perhaps when everyone goes home and forgets about It, It will come back.

The police have set up barricades everywhere, to keep the people from crowding each other into the water and drowning. There have been four deaths by drowning already since the masses have discovered It. I can hardly blame It for leaving them.

With the dark mass gone and the children, or rather parakeets, gone, I am now able to concentrate on repairing my weapon. The police have several vehicles parked on the sand. If I could only get close enough, there is so much confusion that I might be able to steal some tools.

Authority: "Answer the question, Mr. Barker. What were you doing on Dram Street at 3 in the morning of the night in question?"

Barker: "Well, to tell you the truth, I went down there to see if I could pick up a little something. . . ."

A: "I'm afraid that's a little vague."

B: "I was 'on the prowl' if you prefer."

A: "Do you mean you were looking for a woman?"

B: "Yes."

A: "Yes, I suppose young men are inclined towards that sort of thing. So what happened then?"

B: "Well, I wasn't having much luck, and I was about to give up and go home, back to the hotel that is, when I saw this strange thing coming around the corner. It was massive—at least a hundred feet high—a solid, shapeless mass, black as the night and glistening with moisture. It had seaweed stuck to its sides, and shells and barnacles and shit. It slowly oozed down the street, or rather up, heading inland. It didn't try to hurt me; in fact it failed to notice me at all, although I did see it consume a stray alley cat that got in its way. It let out a low, eerie groan, and turned when it came to Crux. I gave it time to get a ways ahead of me, then ran to the corner and peeked around. You know that old warehouse on Crux that was being rebuilt; they were making it into some sort of amusement house called the Flea Circus. Well, when the thing got to that building, a huge door on the side opened and in it slid. Of course I told no one. I couldn't go to the police, and at that time I had no one in my confidence."

# Chapter 38
## News Releafe

(GOLETA) Aug. 9th. After extensive research, investigation, and consultation with scientific experts, Police Chief Beetlebaulm has released a statement confirming the existence of "an alien creature," the rumored "dark mass at the end of the beach." Citizens are cautioned against panic, states Beetlebaulm, as "there is no evidence that the creature is aggressive, and in fact his flight from the Carpinteria Beach area seems to indicate timidity and seclusiveness on the part of the thing." Police authorities have declared a state of martial law. The beach areas of Goleta Shores and Carpinteria Beach are off-limits to all citizens. Police request that this order be respected by all citizens. There is a ten o'clock curfew in effect in the city of Goleta itself. Police believe that the creature may be hiding somewhere in the downtown area and a building-by-building search is being currently conducted in the mile-square area bordered by Dram St. on the north, Crux on the east, Fingle on the south, and the docks on the west. Anyone with information about the creature's nature and habits or present location is urged to contact Police Chief Beetlebaulm immediately. For leaving a one-inch-thick, twenty-foot-wide trail of slime across Highway One, the creature is officially being sought to answer to charges of malicious littering, a felony in Santa Barbara County. Anyone concealing information about the creature will be charged with conspiring to aid and abet a felon. Police Chief Beetlebaulm ended his statement to the press by saying, "There is absolutely nothing to be afraid of. We have the entire situation under control."

# Chapter 39
## The Balcony Scene

I'm standing at the balcony railing right outside the door to our room on the 2$^{nd}$ floor of the Goleta Hotel, gazing down at Paul in the pool who is doing the 19$^{th}$ of his daily series of 20 laps in the pool, to keep his lungs in shape for playing the trumpet. Lying in the sun in a deck chair to the left of the pool is the same young prostitute whom I saw the other day when I was swimming. She is reading the same book as before. She seems to be the intellectual of the group of 33 wayward girls from Kansas. Before coming upstairs, I passed by her as she was reading, and asked her what the book was about. All I could get out of her was that it's about a high-school boy with a deity complex who identifies with the worm he dissects in his biology class. She's not very friendly at all. I wonder how she even managed becoming a wayward girl in the first place.

# Chapter 40
## On the Lam

There's a rumor going about in Goleta that the Thing (as the people have begun calling it) has gone on a tremendous crash diet, bought a large blue suit, put on sunglasses, and got a job at J. C. Penney selling men's underwear in the mezzanine. Afraid of the police, It's trying to lead a quiet, productive life incognito.

Others claim that It's a pigeon that got caught in an oil slick and suffered from the snowball effect when rolled up and down the shore by the tides. Which accounts for its large size, apparent lack of shape, and sticky black appearance.

No rumor yet has accounted for the eyewitnesses' reports that It grew larger and smaller in an oscillating manner while living its solitary existence on the beach at Carpinteria.

# Chapter 41
## Author's Note

[There occurs next a long and gross orgy scene between the 33 wayward girls and the ambiguous "I" of the story, which the author on 2nd thought believed properly left out of the finished manuscript. Any reader consumed by curiosity may contact the author at his home and be shown this section. The gist of it is that there is a party in a vacant room at the Goleta Hotel where the hero and the whores engage in illegal and indecent activities. But the author grew bored with it all.]

# Chapter 42
## Mrs. Ghast Serves Tea

I was cleaning the lenses on my new stereoscopic microscope when Mrs. Ghast came in with a tray of tea. "It's getting frightfully dark out lately," she said.

"Hmm, yes . . . I noticed." The right eyepiece had a stubborn smudge on it. "Would you hand me another of those lens tissues, Mrs. Ghast?"

"Certainly." She handed it to me and I took it from her without looking up. "You're preoccupied with something, aren't you? What is it?"

"Oh it's nothing, really," I said with a sigh, taking a long draught of tea. I leaned back in the chair, filled my pipe, and lit it, sending delicate wreaths of smoke up into the air above my head.

"What is it? It's got you all tensed up," she said, sitting on the arm of the chair.

"Well . . . it's the murders. Not the crimes themselves, they're no problem at all. I shall have them solved in no time at all, if — that's a big if — *if* the criminal continues in the same manner he has been. But this is what's got me worried—I've been studying the man, indirectly of course, studying his mind. And with a little bit more time, I'd be able to outguess him, and I'd have him. But something's gone wrong. I've never met the man . . . but I believe . . . I believe he's going mad."

"But aren't all killers mad, dear?"

"Yes, of course, in society's sense. They're sick. But you see, up till now he's been methodical; there's been a pattern, a sort of code to his thoughts and methods. With a little more study, I could break that code, and I would be one step ahead of him. But he now appears to be losing rationality; his murders are no longer methodical. . . . He's going insane, and I shall not be able to even guess what his next move will be. . . . So close, and now he's slipping out of my grasp. . . ."

Mrs. Ghast quietly sipped her tea.

"Oh," I said, apologetically, "I'm sorry for talking shop, dear. But it does wear hard on me, to be so close to success, and then . . . this."

We both sat in a rather black mood listening to the merciless rain.

# Chapter 43
## The Great Ship

We enter at night through a steel-walled tunnel. The main vault of the ship is a long, narrow cavern extending into the darkness as it curves the horizon. Innumerable smaller caves or rooms branch off from this hull. The ship is made of stone and dirt, and sails under the ocean floor. Stalactites support a feeble lighting system, and small speakers housed in the ceiling's coffers serve as the ship's P.A. system.

Once inside, I follow room after room, branch after branch, corridor after corridor, until I am safely obscured in the ship's massive earthen body. When the ship begins to sail there is the sound of scraping rock. The weight of the sea is above us. The floors are dirt and I wiggle my toes in the cool, dry dust. Fossil hunters ravage the hallways, uncovering primordial fish in sandstone and slate slabs. No word yet from Madrid.

# Chapter 44
## The Private Eye & the Midnight Oil

I sat up half the night going through every recent Goleta newspaper I could find with a fine tooth comb.

"Maybe there's some pattern yet," I mumbled to Mrs. Ghast who was dropping off to sleep on the sofa as I laboured at my desk. "Ah ha! Another!" I snipped out the article with my scissors.

No real pattern had emerged yet, but I had nonetheless collected a large body of strange incidents which seemed strangely and sinisterly related. I saved all the newspaper stories about the Thing as well as accounts of anything else out of the ordinary. In addition, I had interviewed dozens of Goleta citizens in the past twenty-four hours, gleaning from them both eyewitness testimonies and rumours.

Item—rumour that the Thing was fired from its job at J. C. Penney when discovered in the act of feeling up a salesgirl in the stockroom. The young lady is a graduate student in biology, very active in the ecological movement. She is the daughter of a carnival promoter, the owner and operator of the Flea Circus, a fun house and theatre of the low arts on Crux St., not open for business yet.

Item—interview with Professor James Philquist Morehouse, eccentric atomic physicist & religious fanatic. Conducted at his secluded home high atop Mount Fender: "I tell you, lad, the world is getting darker. There's just not as much light anymore. I first started noticing it a few years ago. It was just a suspicion, so I began running tests. The first year, the amount of light out in the middle of the day dropped from 99% of what it should be to 87%. The second year, it dropped even more drastically, from the 87% of the previous year to an astounding 54%. That was six months ago. The first three months of the last six-month period, it dropped from 54% to 33%. Well, for the next two months it stayed pretty well around 33%, 32%. Once, it even rose to 34. But!—and this is what's really got me scared—in the last month, it dropped from the steady 33% to a terrifying 13%! And the terrifying thing is, no one has even noticed! Nothing about it in the papers! I've contacted every scientific agency and journal in America, and none of them will even listen to me, let alone publish my findings! Even the federal government laughs at me. They all say I'm just a crank. . . . Why, it's gotten so bad that I have to go about in the middle of the day with a candle or lantern. My eyes are bad, and I just can't make my way around without a light in these dim days. I finally found someone who would publish my findings, a starving printer in Athens. I sent him my paper. It was to come out this week, a small pamphlet affair with an attractive red paper cover. He was to send me 300 copies. I received one. Here it is—torn to shreds, covered with blood. I received notice yesterday that the poor man—he left a widow and five children—was accidentally killed when an American bomber en route to Vietnam mistakenly dropped its entire payload on his printing shop. Of course, the 299 other copies were destroyed, along with the original paper on my findings. How this one got to me, as mutilated as it is, I'll never know. I was going to rewrite the report, but my house was broken into as I slept last night, and all my notes and equipment were stolen. These are very dark days. . . ."

Item—In the business section of the *New York Times*, auto industry representatives report that car sales of white autos have increased 400%.

Item—542 inches of rain this past month, as compared to a twenty-five year average for this area and for this time of year of 13 inches.

Item—Harvey's Five and Dime on Dram reports a tremendous boom in sales of candles, flashlights, cigarette lighters, flares, and miners' headlamps.

Item—Bishop Godsend reports that church attendance is down to 1% of normal but that those citizens attending have almost invariably conferred with him in private about frightening apocalyptic visions. During a personal field trip to the church (1st Saint John's Holy Cathedral of Goleta) I witnessed only two men at 12 o'clock mass, both in long white robes, with odd, halo-like spheres of radiant gold around their heads. I also noticed a radiant light emanating from the church, which made it the only structure actually visible on Dram, although it was midday.

Item—Construction workers on Crux St. unearthed a human body, male, about 30 years of age, nailed to a wooden cross. Archæologists of the Goleta Center for the Study of Old Things were contacted, and the corpse was removed to the center for further study. Sometime on the 3rd day the specimen disappeared. Police were brought in and are now investigating.

Item—Police reported in the *Goleta Gazetteer Independent Liberty Sun News* that downtown Goleta is currently being plagued by mass suicides. 379 persons perished by their own hand just yesterday. Police expect the trend to die down as the novelty wears off.

There were hundreds of such cases. Something was definitely in the air. I leaned back from my desk, lit my pipe, and asked Mrs. Ghast, who was now completely asleep, "What does it all add up to?"

# Chapter 45
## On the Beach

It's gotten quite dark here lately. All I can really see on the beach anymore is the phosphorescence, which is normally only visible in the evening. This dimness interferes with my tool-searching work. Besides, the police have all gone home now, and taken their trucks and machines with them, so my hopes of stealing some tools off them are now spoiled. I suppose it doesn't really matter if my gun is fixed just now or not. I get lost nowadays when I go out, so I keep pretty much to the bombed-out apartment. I like to look out the window mornings and watch the green glow as the waves roll in. I wonder if the dark mass will return. I miss It.

# Chapter 46
## The Flea Circus

A death at the Flea Circus results in the willful suspension of disbelief. High-school revolutionaries are chewing on chocolate cigars as poolside women's breasts jostle like red balloons. There is no word from Madrid as I await the arrival of tools. Coming, always coming. I am comforted to think that there are so many possibilities. Riding through L.A. after the repeated rejection of my first novel, I actually expect to see a magnificent dirigible rising over the verdant hills. With a good rat-tail file I could get something done.

# Chapter 47
## Fiat Lux

I'm beginning to see (or rather, not see) that the professor is right about it being darker than usual. Today I went down Dram on my way to the library to return some books I had used in reference to the case, and I noticed that several people walked right into me. Others stepped off the curb and into the path of oncoming automobiles. I myself walked smack into a street lamp pole (they don't turn them on until 6 in the evening, in accordance with the civic code). I decided against going all the way to the library, because the trip might be too dangerous, considering, and instead went into the nearest hardware store where I purchased a little electric lamp which I have fastened to my deerstalker's cap. At least now I can see where I'm going, although people still run into me on the sidewalk. It seems that they walk about with their eyes closed, as having their eyes open no longer does them any good. Yet none of them seem to notice the darkness. They have simply adjusted themselves to it without even being aware of the fact.

# Chapter 48
## The Bombed Out Apartment

I am lying here in the semi-dark on my hopsack mattress, thumbing through my inventory and smoking good quality San Pedro dope. There is a spot on the floor, a sort of rectangular stain where the oriental wooden chest used to be before they came and took it away. The kids are gone. There are some yellow feathers around the spot, but that is all that remains of them. I will not allow them to exist in that condition; it is much too disgusting. The waves are crashing against the stone embankment beyond my window that faces the beach. My perceptions are high, and I believe I can smell a fresh starfish mixed with the odor of rotting seaweed. I make a notation in the inventory:

—33 girls. unwed mothers, inept whores. Ages 14-18.

One of them walks in.

"Smells groovy," she says.

"How did you find this place?"

"Saw the light. You really should be more discreet," she says, lacing her fingers under her swollen abdomen. I give her a questioning look. "I mean the pigs," she says.

"Oh. Don't worry. No chance of a bust here. Too far from the town. They have a very small police force in Goleta. Can't waste it on dopers. They're busy trying to bust a myth for littering, and keeping an eye on your 32 sisters."

"Ain't my fucking sisters."

I think that over. "What are you doing so far from the hotel, anyway?"

"Oh," she says. Her nose crinkles and then she laughs. "The crapper's busted in the hotel. Came out here to squirt in the bushes. Saw the glow from your pipe."

By this time she is sitting on the other end of my hopsack mattress. I'm sitting on my end, leaning against the wall and keeping my eye on the spot where the cedar chest used to be. She's wearing a wine-colored satin gown that reaches to her ankles, but it's split up the front to the crotch. She's sitting cross-legged and I can see she hasn't any underwear on. I offer her the pipe. She takes a deep hit.

"We're going to the seashore tomorrow," she says.

"You and the other girls?"

"Yeah, in the bus. Wanna come?"

"Oh, no thanks. I have to help my friend Paul with his music practice."

"Oh wow, is he in a rock group?"

"No. He's a trumpet player with the Lakewood Drum and Bugle Corps. He's really very good though."

"What do they do?" she asks without interest.

"Oh, they march and play, in parades and competitions and stuff."

"I wouldn't be interested in stuff like that."

We sit for a long time, passing the pipe back and forth, and after a while she raises her dress up around her waist and opens her legs even wider.

"Wanna ball?" she asks.

I crush her to death with a large Styrofoam boulder.

# Chapter 49
## It

It was really worried. There was a $10,000 reward being offered for information leading to the arrest of "The Thing." It sat in the park all day, dressed in its large blue suit, wearing its sunglasses, fretting and feeding the pigeons bread crumbs from out of a wrinkled brown paper bag. It wanted a quiet, respectable job somewhere. Something that the police would never suspect and that would yield a meager but satisfactory wage. It could take up foreign-stamp collecting on a modest scale. It would never associate with anyone, except at stamp-collecting conventions. By living a solitary and anonymous existence, It could wait out the seven years until the statute of limitations ran out. Then It could bare its breast to the world and walk proudly with its head up high. It could start a philately museum in San Diego.

Finally, after wearing out the soles of its large, new shoes going from business to business looking for a job, It secured a position at a stationery store, writing greeting-card verse. It was very careful to "tread lightly," fearing betrayal and subsequent arrest. It lived in fear, but looked forward with hope to the day seven years hence when It would be free.

# Chapter 50
## Aboard the Great Dirt Ship

The ancient man sits cross-legged in the dirt. Mineral water drips onto his head from the stalactite above, and off his fingertips into the dust. His breath smells of fish and his teeth are rotted brown. I bum a cigarette off him and he divines my future by examining the book of matches.

The ship moves slowly with the continuous noise of grating rock. We sail for hundreds of hours in one long, cold, uncomfortable night punctuated by endless cups of coffee, chain-smoking, gum-chewing, and anonymous calls for me from out of state, passing through eras and epochs and ages. In the $500^{th}$ hour I get butterflies in my stomach when it is announced over the loudspeaker that we have just pre-dated all known geological time. A hubbub of newsmen.

The archæologists unearth the crushed remains of what appears to be a pregnant female anthropoid. Clutched to the creature's rib cage is a crumbling sheaf of papers. I pry it from the ossified fingers. It is a book, very old. The pages crumble into pieces as I turn them, examining the curious handwriting on them. It is my inventory. I decide to return to the snack bar for another cup of coffee.

# Chapter 51
## Broadfide

POST
NO
BILLS

# Chapter 52
## Mrs. Ghaſt's Appeal

The pattern remained beyond my grasp. Because of her distraċting charms, I found it hard to work around Mrs. Ghast; I needed time to be alone and ponder the case. I rose from the armchair in her parlour after dinner and announced that I was going down to "the rooms."

"Whatever for?" she asked in surprise.

"Have to stay up tonight, think this thing through."

"Must you go down there? Can't you stay here? It'll be so bloody miserable down there. . . ." She was right; her home is relatively high on Dram (about halfway up the hill), compared to my rooms at #1 Lower Dram, the very base of the street, and so drier and therefore warmer. I hadn't been home in days, but I reasoned that the rain running down Dram would have colleċted at the base of the street. In addition to this, the sea was normally almost at my door, and that at low tide. With reports over the wireless of a gale at sea a few miles off the coast of Goleta, it was going to be a rough night.

"I suppose you're right," I said. "But still I feel I must be off . . . just tonight at least . . . if I'm going to solve this case."

"But can't you think here?" There was a pleading look in her eyes. "I shall go to bed early, and you'll have the whole place to yourself. Couldn't you?"

"No, I'm sorry. Not tonight, it's impossible. I need to be in my office in order to get into the correċt frame of mind for problem solving. Besides, I'd just keep you awake, what with my pacing to and fro, and tea-making—you know the whistling kettle always wakes you. Besides, there are some documents down there I have to look at."

"But there's a storm coming. It'll be terribly cold and wet and windy; won't that distract you?"

"No, I rather think a raging bloody gale might actually aid my meditations. There's nothing like the sound of wind and waves and beating rain outside to put one in the proper frame of mind for late night musing. As for the cold, have you any spare quilts?"

"Oh damn you," she said, realizing that nothing she could say would change my mind. She went and got a large woolen blanket from the cupboard. "This is all I have. I bet they find you frozen in the morning."

"I hardly think so."

# Chapter 53
## Laudanum

When I got down the hill I had to wade through water chest-deep to get to my place at #1 Lower Dram. I had a hell of a time finding the door (which was broken off the hinges by the pressure of the water from outside), as I had been hit by a few waves, and the water short-circuited the electric lamp on my cap, leaving me in the dark. The ground floor, a combination study and consulting room, was flooded knee-deep. I went upstairs, lit the gas lamp, and placed it on the top of the stairs so that the flooded room below was illuminated, and spent a half hour moving all of my waterlogged possessions to the upstairs. The storm was due in an hour or so. I lit a fire and boarded up the shutters, then stacked my soggy books around the fire so that they could slowly dry out. There was nothing left to do but wait for it to come.

The wind began to build up outside. This 2nd story was a sort of roomy attic fitted out to be a laboratory. There were tables covered with old dusty glassware, and the walls were lined with glass cases containing hundreds of vials of chemicals. Suddenly I remembered a bottle of laudanum I had hidden among the vials; it was labeled POTASSIUM FERRICYANIDE to avert suspicion. I took a large dose, wrapped the gray wool blanket around me, and waited for the fury.

# Chapter 54
## Bottom of the Ocean

Three dark tidal waves come in, washing with tremendous force over me and the city of Goleta. I am overpowered by the enormous mass and weight of the water. Then there is a calm and I lie drenched on the beach. Little bubbles of foam are bursting at my mouth. I see the people of the city, half-drowned, pick themselves up and run from the sea on weak legs. I struggle out as far as I can and meet the next three waves head-on, diving through the 40 foot curls and emerging on the long, steep backside slopes. Half a mile out I can see the next group of three—the black curls glistening with chrome silver highlights in the pale sun—and behind them, other triads of waves, hundreds of them emanating from behind the horizon.

I pass through the next three waves, forcing myself out farther against the colossal pull of the waves towards the shore. When I am far enough out, I take advantage of a calm to dive down under. It is frighteningly black and thick with seaweed. I feel my flesh crawl as the writhing tentacles of kelp slither over my face, limbs, and stomach. I have a revulsion to the horrifying depth and blindness but am driven down even deeper by compulsion. Miles under I reach the bottom. The oceans bear down on me with a horrible moaning weight, and living fossils of trilobites eat the flesh off my bones.

# Chapter 55
## News

(GOLETA) May 1st, 1897. Mr. David Barker, noted by Goleta residents as one of the finest private investigators in our fair city by the sea, was found frozen to death this morning in the attic of his flooded offices at #1 Lower Dram St. The tragic discovery was made by Mrs. Elizabeth Ghast of 233 Upper Dram, a widow whom the much-respected detective occasionally consulted in relation to the occult aspects of his cases. Mrs. Ghast, an experienced medium, told police that she made the discovery when she was bringing him down a thermos of soup, as she was aware that he had spent the night in the unheated offices. The entire docks area suffered from violent winds, rain, and surf due to a storm lasting throughout the night, with the Lower Dram area being the hardest hit. According to police, Barker had apparently attempted to keep out the storm by boarding up the windows. Due to the tremendous force of what the Coast Guard called "the worst gale in Goleta's history," the windows of Barker's attic were literally ripped open, and Barker, apparently in a trance-like state induced by a heavy dose of opiate tincture, was soon covered with sea water and quick-frozen by the icy winds as early morning temperatures dropped to a record 40 degrees below zero. Services for the sleuth have not yet been set.

# Chapter 56
## Boogie-Woogie

I am in the lobby of the Goleta Hotel after dinner, seated on the end of a very long sofa; next to me are the remaining 32 wayward girls. There is a Western on the color TV and no one has spoken for 15 minutes. The color is off, but no one will get up to adjust it. Cowboys and horses are chartreuse against livid pink brushlands.

Paul comes down and, as there is no more room on the sofa, sits in an overstuffed chair by the picture window. The pool is throwing scallops of aquamarine light over his face. He can't see the TV from where he sits. He winds his watch.

The pool is empty now, but the water is agitated; someone has been swimming, and there is a trail of footprints and drips leading away from the pool's edge.

Two boys, identical twins, come in. They look 12 but say they are 15. One sits on the far arm of the sofa, and the other indicates with his eyes that he wants to sit on the arm by me, but I have my arm there. I don't move it, but begin drumming my fingers on the Naugahyde, which makes an irritating popping noise.

"Shaddup," one of the whores says. I stop.

Another with strawberry blonde hair says to the kid who wants my arm, "Hey kid, fix the TV, will ya?"

He grins like an idiot. "What for? Nuthin' wrong with it."

"What, are ya blind, kid? The color's all screwed."

"Why don't you fix it yourself?" He sticks his hands into his pockets.

"Come on, pukeface, you're up, fix it, dammit."

He grins and shuffles around.

"Goddamn it, fix it, kid."

"Ah go to hell," he mumbles.

"Goddamn it, shit-kid, do I have to bust you in the fucking mouth?"

He just sneers.

"Goddamn kid . . ." She gets up grumbling to adjust the TV, and as soon as her hand touches the knob, the kid darts for her space on the sofa. She lunges at him and pounds on his shoulder with a tight fist.

"Goddamn it, shit-kid, this is my damn seat."

"Naww, you left it and now it's mine. Quit your damn pounding on me."

"Goddamn, shit-ass kid, I only got up to fix the TV. My seat was saved."

"You left it."

"It was saved."

"Shit, kid . . ." She elbows him in the face, knocking him off the couch and onto the floor, then plops her huge butt into the seat. "Damn kid," she mutters, straightening her blouse and brushing the strands of hair from her face.

He gets up off the floor, walks over to the piano, and starts playing the bass part to a high-powered boogie-woogie. His brother joins in on the high notes. Everyone is very impressed.

"Rattle them bones," says the strawberry blonde.

# Chapter 57
## Air-Conditioned Cafeteria

I am sitting at my table in the cafeteria. It is late afternoon and all of the tables but mine are unoccupied and have been cleared. The waitress comes by with a cart and picks up my trash. With a soapy rag she cleans off my table.

"This section is closed," she says blandly.

"I'm waiting for word from Madrid."

She goes away without wiping my table dry.

# Chapter 58
## Wednefday


In the hospital my clinical lover comes to me, wrapped in antiseptic white sheets. She rubs against me, her body smooth and warm under the linen. This arouses me and I reach out to fondle her breast, but she stops me.

"Did you call Jesus today like I asked you?"

"No," I say, "I just didn't feel like it."

She becomes very angry and exposes herself to me, a branch of bloodied thorns growing out of the sex between her legs.

"Rattle them bones," the strawberry blonde repeats. The twins are pounding out a mean boogie by now. They stand hunched over the piano and rock on their heels in unison as they play. Then they break into "Rock Around the Clock" and the crowd goes wild. Unable to control herself any longer, the strawberry blonde lifts up her dress and begins banging herself off against the piano.

I look around and notice that Paul is gone. I find him in our room upstairs, playing a soft, precise "Carnival of Venice" on his trumpet. The sound of the metronome makes me sleepy and I lie down on the bed; it's one of those soft hotel beds, perfectly made without a wrinkle. I can faintly hear the throbbing bass notes of the piano as I drift off into sleep, a thick, dreamless sleep until just before waking, when I dream I am making love to the Jewish girl in the Swansea Arms Hotel in downtown Long Beach on our honeymoon. It's very good. I'm about to reach my climax, but then she wants to stop.

"It's almost morning and I'm very tired," she says with a yawn as she rolls over onto her side. I ask if we are going to do it again soon. "Of course," she says in a sleepy, angry voice. "You don't think that's the end of your duty as a husband to me, do you?"

"Of course I don't," I say. "I rather hoped we'd do it again."

"Good," she says. "We'll do it again next Thanksgiving."

The dream ends with me feeling gypped.

I get up and take a shower.

# Chapter 60
## Doing Dope Again

Gorillas at dawn couldn't soothe me. I'm feeling low. I want to get loaded. You are a good friend, someone I can trust. You're holding. We roll a giant joint like a cigar in the back of the bus. It doesn't burn well. Then you do something to it and it becomes a torch. Smoke is billowing out of the bus window. It begins to take effect; my arms are cold and heavy. They move slowly and mechanically like cranes. I'm not sure what I'm doing or saying until it happens. I'm speeding. The bus driver is speeding. I'm an amoeba, my heart pumps rapidly in a clear body. You get up to get a transfer. As you walk back to our seat, we stare at each other in perspective: you are small and I am large, and I am small and you are large.

I get off in the back streets of Beverly Hills. I come to an empty residential avenue. It's a row of ominous mansions, all painted white with black trim. I feel very uncomfortable and walk hastily. Suddenly I remember your words: "whorehouse mansions owned by the mafia." I am afraid that someone will come out of one of the houses to try to persuade me in. I start with fright as a man steps out from behind a hedge, but it's only a gardener, swishing the blades of his shears.

Much later, I am crawling over steep mountain crags, trying to keep from falling into the deep white cardboard crevices and inadvertently ruining a new pair of baggy slacks.

I meet you again later in front of the TV; you have become my mother. You try something funny. I leave and you don't see me for days. Later you discover me in the laundry room, playing boogie on the scrub bucket. I'm embarrassed and don't know what to expect next.

# Chapter 61
## Police


Upon the death of Mr. David Barker, private investigator of #1 Lower Dram, Goleta, the City Police Squad For The Protection Of Goleta Citizens From Religious Hokum & Other Nonsense (headed by Police Chief Beetlebaulm) raided Mr. Barker's offices and confiscated 500 pounds of soggy notes from the late detective's files. Beetlebaulm told reporters that the detective was apparently working on a secret case or series of related cases at the time of his accidental death by ice, and that the case or cases were being taken over by the CPSFTPOGCFRH&ON.

# Chapter 62
## News

(MADRID) Sept. 3rd. Prominent archaeologist Sir Richard Wrought, who left his stately home in Goleta earlier this year in order to accompany a select team of distinguished experts to an excavation site in Madrid, shocked the scientific world earlier this week by sending home the team without explanation. The noble doctors Smithe, Jones, Applebaum, Casey & Hernandez arrived by jet early Tuesday morning in New York. All were unavailable for comment except Jones, who agreed to a press conference Wednesday afternoon. Unfortunately, the great Dr. Jones was accidentally run over by a United States Army bulldozer as he left his hotel at about noon Wednesday. Dr. Jones lay in a coma for five hours when he was fatally injured during a mysterious explosion in his ward of the hospital, which killed 4 other patients and seriously injured 43. Police have declined to investigate. According to an anonymous rumor received by the Goleta Gazetteer Independent Liberty Sun News Agency, Sir Richard Wrought has made some sort of major discovery and is continuing to work alone in Madrid. According to the same source, the team was dismissed for security reasons, although, editorially speaking, the Goleta Gazetteer Independent Liberty Sun News Agency can see no reason why the noble doctors Smithe, Applebaum, Casey, Hernandez & the late Dr. Jones should be considered security risks.

# Chapter 63
## Tranſcript

Authority: "And did you love her very much, Mr. Barker?"

Barker: "As deeply as the salt sea."

A: "And what did they do to her, sir?"

B: "They persecuted her, stripped her, stoned her, violated her, disfigured her, left her to rot on the pavement."

A: "And do you still blame them?"

B: "Yes."

A: "And what will you do in revenge?"

B: "I will burn their fine houses."

# Chapter 64
## 500 Pounds of Soggy Notes

Police Chief Beetlebaulm divided the City Police Squad For The Protection Of Goleta Citizens From Religious Hokum & Other Nonsense into several committees, assigned each a specific task, or "station," and began work immediately on the gargantuan job of processing the 500 pounds of soggy notes confiscated from the "Barker Files."

STATION 1—Committee One (a solitary old man, a retired surgeon with amazingly steady hands). Task: To carefully peel the thousands of individual slips of paper apart from one another, slowly working down from the top of the 12 foot stack, one slip at a time. (The notes are so waterlogged that, if not separated from each other with exceeding care, they could easily shred into unintelligible wads of pulp.) Notes are passed on via tweezers to station 2.

STATION 2—Committee Two (an unemployed short-order cook and a young man training to become a computer operator). Task: To thoroughly dry each note over a hot toaster. One man dries, the other keeps pressing down the toaster button as it keeps popping up. Special care required at this station not to burn notes by keeping them over the toaster too long at any one time.

STATION 2A—Committee Three (an eight-year-old with a roll of Scotch Magic Tape). This station intercepts notes passed from station 2 to station 3 that are in need of repair due to poor peeling at station 1. The torn notes are repaired and passed back into the mainstream of notes passing from station 2 to station 3.

STATION 3—Committee Four (a 60-year-old widow who lives in a trailer park and spends her spare time studying handwriting analysis, religious hokum &

other nonsense). Task: to decipher Barker's miserable handwriting and transcribe the notes into typed copy which she passes onto station 4. She makes a carbon duplicate which she passes onto station 5.

STATION 4—Committee Five (Chief Beetle-baulm). Task: to read notes. Also, to decide whether each note should: (1) be forwarded to the FBI, (2) be forwarded to Goleta Police files, (3) be burned by armed guards, or (4) be used to line the bottom of the chief's canary cage.

STATION 5—Committee Six (eleven imported Benedictine monks, none of whom speaks English). Task: Monk One selects and prepares vellum skins; Monks Two through Seven labor all night by candle-light, writing out the notes in manuscript with broad pens and soot-ink; Monk Eight rubricates in red and blue ink; Monk Nine binds the book in calfskin and decorates the boards with curious tools stamped in blind; Monk Ten, traveling day and night on donkey back, delivers the 200 pound volume to the Huntington Library along with letters of introduction from the Pope.

# Chapter 65
## Monk Ten

Monk Ten, who was supposed to travel day and night on donkey back to deliver the 200 pound volume of *Barker's Notes* to the Huntington Library, couldn't resist temptation and stopped on the first evening out of Goleta at the Blue Hogg Inn. He ran up quite a bill, indulging himself in a sumptuous meal of roast pheasant and beef, five bottles of Port, a plug of the best Turkish tobacco, a private room for the night, and three ladies of pleasure, one of whom was a virgin and quite expensive in these parts, and therefore found it necessary to sell his donkey in order to settle with the innkeeper.

He awoke in the morning hungover and abandoned by his bedmates, donkey-less, and in a troubled state of mind wondering how he would ever get to the Huntington Library on foot in time. If he failed to appear in two weeks, Chief Beetlebaulm had assured him, it would be assumed that he had absconded with the book, yet it was a month's journey on foot, at least. And there was the book to carry; one couldn't carry the 200 pound book on foot. The book! Monk Ten cast an eye around the dingy little room. It was gone! The book itself was gone! He jumped out of bed and scrambled around the room, but to no avail. The book was gone and so were his monk's robes. But in their place in the corner were some other articles of clothing. Monk Ten examined them. It was the perfect disguise for evading Chief Beetlebaulm and the CPSFTPOGCFRH&ON. The light blue suit was way too big for even him (a stocky monk), but the sunglasses were ideal. Monk Ten put on the disguise conveniently left by the thief of the book and his robes, and was heading for the door, when he noticed something odd: from the window ledge to the corner where the book had been and from the corner to the door of his room was a sticky, rather slimy black trail upon the floor. It was about five feet wide, looked like a snail's trail except it was black, and smelled like oily fish. Curious, thought Monk Ten, as he lit a candle and left the hotel.

# Chapter 66
## Evil

One note in particular from the "Barker Files" bothered Police Chief Beetlebaulm to such a degree that, rather than forward it to the police files or FBI, or burn it as blasphemous, or use it to line the bottom of his canary cage, he instead folded it up and hid it in the inside lining of his long underwear. At night, in the secrecy of his bed, he would take it out and read it over and over again by flashlight. He wasn't sure what it meant, but he was determined that it mustn't fall into the hands of the City Police Squad For The Protection Of Goleta Citizens From Religious Hokum & Other Nonsense. It both frightened and fascinated him; he had no idea what relation it bore to the series of murders Barker was working on, yet it was apparently of great significance in Barker's eyes, as the late detective had written across the top of the page in red ink, "Ah ha!"

### NOTE # 15639

—went to Sir Rds Library and borrowed several books thru his daughter's courtesy. Amongst them, found this, p. 118 of St. Thomas' Fiat Lux, 1553:

"Of Darkenesse and Beasts, there fore, let it suffyce to say that they are one unto the other and coum together. The Antients have wrytten of Euil times that the skies grew dayly dark, but onely visible was this fackt to the vvise and goode at heart. Also is told a history of a Beast of Darkenesse risen from the Sea by God Almiqhtye on High to stalk the lande and scourge the Citys of ther Euil by Pestilents."

# Chapter 67
## The Coastal Route

The Thing, disguised as Monk Ten in long brown robes, traveled south along the beach en route to the Huntington Library with the 200 pound volume of *Barker's Notes*. It chose the coastal route so that It might return to the sea in case of emergency. There were seldom any reports about Itself in the papers anymore, yet It was sure that the Goleta Police were still after It for the littering rap.

# Chapter 68
## Backſtage at the Flea Circus

They are hawking tickets in the halls of the Goleta Hotel at midnight. Like a fool, I buy one. The seller takes my money and quickly leaves via the fire escape. I must go at once it says on the ticket. A short man in a trench coat points the way, his up-turned collar covering his mouth and nose. A car door opens at the base of the stairs. I get in; we drive away into the dark. I change my mind. I don't want to go to the Flea Circus, but I'm embarrassed to tell them. They would have to stop the car specially for me. And refund my money. If they give refunds. I'd be willing to sacrifice the amount of the ticket. I feel unsafe. My shadowy companions do not speak. It begins to rain again.

"You can let me out here," I say, reaching for the door handle.

"Why . . . don't you want to see the show, my friend?"

"Ah . . . I really shouldn't have bought that ticket. I've got work to do back at the hotel. I really should get back. . . ."

"But my friend, how can we possibly allow you to miss the show? It's not very often that the Flea Circus comes to town. It would be very poor of us as your hosts to allow you to miss the show."

"Besides, I really couldn't afford the price of the ticket. . . ."

*"There are no refunds at the Flea Circus!"*

"Well what's done is done." Who are these people? Where are they taking me? I don't want to go to the Flea Circus. I paid for this. "Hey look, you guys. You can keep the money, you can have the ticket. I really gotta get back to the hotel. My friend Paul will be worried sick. Why don't you just let me out here?"

"But Mr. Barker, it's raining out. We can't possibly let you out in this miserable weather. We can't assume responsibility for what might happen to you out there. After all, you might catch cold. And besides, this isn't the best part of town. It's not safe to be out on the streets at this hour. We really cannot allow it."

"No really, I'll be all right. I'll hitch a ride home. I'll walk. I don't mind. Really. I love to walk in the rain. I never catch cold. My friend is probably worried sick. I'm tired. I really must get back to the hotel; why don't you guys just let me out here and go on without me? I always talk during shows. I'm a heckler. I fall asleep and snore. I'm really a drag to be with. You guys'd have a lot more fun without me along to ruin your evening."

"Mr. Barker . . . there is no point discussing it any further. *Everyone must go to the Flea Circus sooner or later!*"

Now I'm really screwed. I should never have bought that ticket. Goddamn bleeding heart, that's what I am. Thought I was doing the wretch a favor. The pimp. The goddamn pimp. Just leading me on. I played right into his hands. Innocent son of a bitch I am. Goddamn fool. Everyone takes me for a ride. But what do they want with me? What do the fucking perverts want? I don't have any money. Oh no! White slavery! White queer slavery! I gotta get the living fuck out of here! Dirty leering hands on my body!

೦೪

I grabbed the door handle and pushed outward with all my weight. The next thing I knew I was lying on the street, tasting the warmth of blood in my mouth. I was stunned by the impact and my skin stung with abrasions. I had no idea how badly I was hurt. I looked up and saw the car heading back towards me. I thought of broken bones and wondered if I could move. A hand reached out of the darkness and helped me to my feet.

"This way," the voice said. We ducked into an alley as the car sped by. I heard it screeching on the wet street as it turned around again to come after us, and we ran like mad down the alley, slipping and stumbling because of the rain and dark. "Here," the voice said, leading me down cellar stairs. He unlocked the door and slammed it shut after us. We leaned against it in complete blackness, breathing hard and shivering with fear and cold. We heard the car go by the door several times and then it was gone.

"Be all right now," the voice said. I heard him fumble and then strike a match. "They're gone now." I only saw his back. He was wearing a large blue suit. He walked over to the table and lit a lamp. He huddled over it as he talked. "I was on my way back from the Water Works on Crux when I saw you jump from the car. I'd know that car anywhere. Figured you were in trouble. Always lend a helping hand, that used to be our motto in the Order."

"Yes, I was sort of in trouble. Thank you very much."

"Think nothing of it."

"No really, I was in quite a jam."

He suddenly swung around, and I saw his face for the first time. It was thin and old, and he had a long, full red beard. "Probably wonder what I was doing up at the Water Works this time a night, eh?"

"No, hadn't even thought of it."

"Don't tell me that. Young men are always curious."

"Well, now that I think of it, it is a little odd."

"What do they have at the Water Works?"

"Water, I guess."

"Of course they do! What else?"

"Water . . . ah . . ."

"What do they keep the water in?"

"I dunno, what?"

"Use your mind, boy! What?"

"Ah . . . vats, I guess."

"And what else? Vats and what else?"

"I don't know. Really I don't."

"Pipes!"

"Yeah?"

"Damn right! Pipes!" He walked over to me and stood so that we were eye to eye and he breathed in my face. "And what are pipes made of?"

"Ah, metal . . . lead."

"Lead! Jesus! We'd all be dead if they were made of lead, boy! What are they made of?"

"I don't know."

He put his hand on my shoulder and drew me near to him, whispering in my ear:

"Brass. Brass!"

"Yeah?"

"Damn right. Brass. I steal plumbing. Brass is an expensive metal. At night, I slip into the Water Works and every night I take one section of plumbing. I bring it here." He pointed to the room, which, now that I noticed it, was loaded with brass plumbing fixtures. They gleamed a yellowish orange in the dimness of the room. "A man has to make an honest living."

"What do you do with it all?"

"Sell it. Bit by bit."

"I mean who do you sell stolen brass to? The black market?"

"Oh no. I never deal with unreputables. I sell it back to the Water Works. They love me. I have a small stock but I always seem to have just the parts they need. I told them they should get a watchdog or something. Want a drink?" He opened the cupboard and took out a bottle of wine.

We sat at the table, drinking out of dusty glasses.

"I know all about you," he said.

"Huh?"

"I said I know all about you."

"What do you know about me?"

"Well, for instance, I know you're looking for tools."

"Oh yeah?" I said, laughing. "How can you tell?"

"It's written all over your face."

"Hmm . . . that's really odd."

"That's not all."

"What else?"

"Well . . . I know about when you crossed the barrier on the beach and about the dark mass at the end of the beach, the one that kept receding."

"Well I'll be damned. Jesus, that's weird. Read it in the papers, did you?"

"Oh no, was there something about it?"

"Big write-up . . . on the dark mass, that is, not on me. Sure you didn't read it in the papers?"

"Positive."

"Well, how'd you know?"

"It's written all over your face."

"That's too damn weird."

"Not at all. There's more. For example, the 33$^{rd}$ prostitute, and what you did to her."

"Do you think less of me for it?"

"No affair of mine. Besides, that's in the past and really doesn't matter so much now. Can't change what's already happened. No sense worrying about it."

"Yeah, that's true in a sense."

We sat silently drinking and eyeballing each other. I was dying to get to a mirror and see what exactly was written on my face. I refilled my glass.

"Say," I said, "you haven't by any chance read my inventory, have you?"

"No, I swear, it's simply written on your face."

"Huh, I'll be damned."

"Yes."

I showed up at the Goleta Hotel at 6 o'clock the

next morning, my clothes torn and blood-stained. In the pocket of my coat I found a piece of brass pipe. Paul asked where I had been and what on earth had happened to me. I was almost too tired to answer him; all I wanted was a bath and Band-Aids and sleep. I took a towel from my suitcase and stumbled into the bathroom.

"Where have you been?" Paul asked again through the door.

"I've been to the Flea Circus."

# Chapter 69
## Revelation

Chief Beetlebaulm was sitting on the toilet masturbating one morning when he received a special delivery telegram from Madrid:

Dear Boy,
Still digging and haven't uncovered the TRUTH yet, but came up with this small tidbit which may be of some use to you. It appears that our Beastly Friend of Darkness somehow has overtaken the identity of Monk #10. How deeply the Benedictine is involved in this criminal matter remains to be seen. However, you may alert your men to be on the lookout for a non-English speaking fellow in a large blue suit and dark glasses, as I am now convinced that such a costume is the manner in which the Thing chose to attire his person before taking on the habit of dear Mother Church. I suspect that some sort of exchange of garments has taken place, as such is the kind of solution that presents itself to the simple mind of the desperado. Therefore, assume that the Monster has on the monk's robes and the monk has on the Monster's large blue suit. Assume further that the Beast has also taken on the duties of Monk #10, and is probably en route to the Huntington Library with the 200 pound book of Barker's Notes. Feeling very insecure (and whom amongst us wouldn't, facing a felony rap for malicious littering?), the Thing would probably decide to travel along the coast, where It could seek refuge in the sea if It blew cover. Do you remember reports you received late last week that a vagrant was sighted walking northward along Carpinteria Beach, apparently in search of the Dark Mass at the end of the beach? Well, assuming that the Dark Mass is traveling southward along the beach and that the vagrant is traveling northward along the same beach, it seems safe to conjecture that they will cross paths. I conjectured thus and therefore sent one of my most trusted agents to the scene. He reports that the two suspects rendezvoused on the beach at approximately

11:00 last night. In the words of the agent: "They met, seemed to recognize each other, spoke for about fifteen minutes, the Thing doing most of the talking, although I was unfortunately too far away at my observation point to overhear the conversation. Then they both undressed. The Beast remained nude, whereas the vagrant put on the monk's robes and took up the large book. The Thing then disappeared into the brush towards the City of Goleta, and the vagrant changed course and headed southward down the beach." It seems, therefore, my dear Chief, that the Thing is up to his old tricks of hiding in the backstreets of Goleta. Now all that remains is to locate the Benedictine and the vagrant and question them both regarding the future plans of the Thing. They may be able to give us information that will be of great value in locating and prosecuting the Thing. Also, I have reason to suspect that the identity of the vagrant might be none other than a certain Mr. Barker, a deranged labourer reported AWOL from a governmental tool factory. According to an all-points bulletin just handed to me less than an hour ago, this Barker character went berserk at the Federal Tool Factory, where he has been employed as an assembly-line man for the last 2 years, and clubbed to death 5 of his supervisors with a cast-iron water pistol. He escaped and has been desperately sought by the FBI for the duration of the intervening month. If this pans out and the vagrant is Barker, we may have enough circumstantial evidence to hang both him and the Thing for the Goleta Whore Slayings. We would both benefit from a conviction, so get your ass in gear.

> Respectfully,
> Sir Richard Wrought
> June 18th, 1865
> Black Pit Caverns,
> Madrid

# Chapter 70
## Politics

I'm sitting here in our room at the Goleta Hotel, with a terrible hangover headache, and I have to read 100 pages of logarithm tables for school. I decide that my abortive ride to the Flea Circus last night didn't happen; it was a dead end of the subconscious, a blind-alley scene in the book.

You are a revolutionary. You burst into the room with tommy guns and clutch me by the throat, screaming, "Nerd! Fucking nerd!"

I surrender. "Please," I say, "I'm only a poor poet waiting for word from Madrid."

"Aw shit!" you say, shoving me against the dresser and heading for the door.

"Wait," I say.

"What is it now?"

"Do you have any tools on you?"

"Tools? Fuck off, cocksucker!" You slam the door shut behind you after spitting on the WELCOME mat.

# Chapter 71
## After Hours at the Flea Circus

I came to be there quite naturally. The Manikin and the Ringmaster were standing in a circle of sawdust. I couldn't make out every word. Their speech had a rhythm like that of field sparrows.

"Whatever happened to him?" the Ringmaster said in his slow, deep voice. The Manikin shuffled with pigeon-toes; his eyes were wild and the gawky blonde hair stuck out of his head in random clumps. He had a weak chin and a high voice like a spastic. I knew right away he was a potential rock star.

"I dun rightly recawl."

"Well, you knew him, didn't you?"

"Yeah, yeah," he said, breaking into a wide squinting smile. "He was my first roommate."

"Yup, I always wonder what became of him."

"Wawl . . . they comes and goes. They comes and they goes."

"Probably went to Metro. . . ."

# Chapter 72
## Score

Paul's father had to drive into town on business as usual and we decided to go with him. After we swam in the afternoons, we sat down by the pool and let the sun dry us off. Our hair would get so dry that it blew around and didn't comb and so Paul would bring out the Score. We rubbed it through our hair and then it combed into place so that if we went out to dinner or a movie or if we just sat around all evening in the lobby it would look okay. Soon the Score was almost empty and we had to get a new tube.

Paul's father parked in front of the real-estate office and we got out. There was no furniture in the office, only freshly painted walls and large plate-glass windows. Paul went to the drugstore down the street to get the tube of Score and some stamps, and I went looking for tools.

I went walking down the street looking for a tool store, but I thought I was sitting in the air-conditioned cafeteria listening to the jukebox, drinking a cup of black coffee, and smoking menthol cigarettes. The record was "Sally Go Round the Roses" by I forget who, and when it was over the waitress came by and wiped my table dry.

# Chapter 73
## The Old Shell Game

I knocked on the ocean. "How's things in there?"

"All us oysters doing our best."

The Ocean Company sends me an extra large bill this month, charging me for nine 40 foot tidal waves, a gale, and a quarter-mile coral reef, all of which I'm sure I never used. I go to the Goleta branch of the Ocean Company to inquire. The woman is snotty:

"Our billing computers never make a mistake."

"I never used these waves. Really. I never even heard of them. And this coral reef. Good God! That's the sort of thing a person would remember using!"

"Let me get your record. What is your beach, Mr. Barker?"

"Ah . . . Carpinteria, near the fruit-picking fields."

She goes to a file cabinet and takes out a cream-colored folder.

"This address, sir, is it a residence?"

"You mean do I live there?"

"Mmm—yes, sir."

"Uh-huh."

"And are you still employed at the library?"

"Yes."

"How long have you been employed there, sir?"

"Three years, this December."

She makes some notations on my record, then looks up at me with a pinched nose and rhinestone-studded glasses hanging from a gold-filled chain around her neck.

"Well . . . we'll deduct these charges from your bill for the time being. We'll notify you after we make an investigation into the charges. That's five dollars and sixty-eight cents, please."

I give her a ten and she gives me back four sand dollars, three trilobites, and two kelp polyps for change.

# Chapter 74
## Infomnia

I spend a restless night flopping from side to side on my sweaty bed in the Goleta Hotel. A neon sign across the road from my window blinks *red-green-red-green* and in rhythm to it, I am picturing in my mind *hammer-file-hammer-file*. . . . The radium dials on my watch say 2:15 and at last I fall asleep, dreaming of a white-gray rat-tail file fresh from the hardware store, beautifully cast without a gouge or abrasion on its slender tapered body. There is not even a single bit of dirt caught under any of its sharp new teeth. It is a pièce de résistance among tools.

## Chapter 75
## My Death


I die. The weather is terrible. We are traveling the coast. There is perpetual night. We are taking soup in a hovel out of the rain. I feel like a child.

You are offended by my innocence. "I know you," you say. "You are not new, you are old."

I sip my broth slowly, savoring the hot vegetables that lie in the bottom of the bowl. "You are very old," I say.

You grimace bitterly. "Yes, I am." You go off into the rain, bundled in thick, coarse rags. He will return before morning, someone says.

James Joyce comes at midnight, carrying the *Book of Kells*. He tells us of his journey from Iona:

"The vandals are everywhere; the Continent is in ruin, but Dublin is safe."

# Chapter 76
## The Mortician's Art

They removed the body of the strawberry blonde whore from the end of the piano. It was shrouded in tinfoil and sent back to the kitchen of her parents' home in Kansas. The groom wore Appaloosa hide and quickly became 23. His twin brother served as best man. They raised three syphilitic children. He bought a 1958 Buick and she got a job as a beauty operator. Their story ends before it begins.

The pages of the *Book of God* are coming out. We spend all night Scotch-taping them back in.

A clean-cut young man takes a table in the air-conditioned cafeteria and sits down to chocolate cream pie. Somewhere in 1930 New York City Professor Seagull is making tomato ketchup soup from hot tea water in an all-night cafe. The pages of his *Oral History* blow across the land.

# Chapter 77
## Before the Show Begins

After swimming all afternoon, Paul and I both take showers to get the chlorine off of us. Then I use the Score to comb my long hair back. I wear a brown pullover sweater and the one pair of slacks I brought.

We get to the Goleta Athenæum Theatre a half hour before the movie is to start. The auditorium has floor-to-ceiling curtains all around the walls. There is a soft indirect lighting on the curtains so that it looks like twilight in the theatre, and soft music is coming from the speakers behind the screen. I feel like I'm in ancient Greece. The sun has just gone down and a mild breeze is blowing through the columns. My clinical goddess comes to me, draped in an airy linen gown. She floats in through the curtains under the green EXIT light and sits in the seat next to me. They are reclining seats and she pushes mine back and rests her head on my chest. Her hair smells like jasmine; it is rich brown and flows over her shoulders and into my lap.

"A kiss?" I ask.

"No."

"Why not?"

"First . . . I want to ask you something."

"What?"

She looks up at me with her beautiful, piercing eyes. She touches my lip with her finger. "Love me, right?"

"Yes, of course. You know I do."

"Even though you love me very much—you do love me very much, don't you?"

"Yes I do."

"Even though you love me very much, if Jesus told you to kill me, would you?"

"No."

"But what if that's what he wanted you to do?"

"He wouldn't."

"But what if he did?"

"But he wouldn't."

"But if he *did*, wouldn't you?"

"Come on, kiss me."

"No—not until you say you would."

"But I can't. It's insanity."

"Then I can't kiss you."

I agree to murder on divine command and she gives her warm mouth to me. Consummation occurs several thousand years later.

# Chapter 78
## News if You Choofe Will Give You the Blues

(GOLETA) Sept 25th. Citizens in the vicinity of Crux Street report hearing strange noises in the wee hours of the morning, according to Chief Beetlebaulm of the Goleta City Police Force. Descriptions of the noises volunteered by citizens range from "definitely the sound of large slabs of stone rubbing against one another" to "the eerie cry of human anguish and mortification." Police as of yet have no official explanation for the phenomenon, but believe that the rumors may have the same source as those received a few weeks ago dealing with a supposed sea monster. Chief Beetlebaulm reminds citizens that the submitting of false reports to the police is a misdemeanor punishable by castration and that such tricksterism greatly interferes with the Goleta City Police Force in its pursuit of the classic American goal of justice, peace, law and order, liberty, and the pursuit of happiness.

# Chapter 79
## Gardenias

Something has gone foul. I move in circles with failure written on my lips. The gardenias are rotting; it is the putrid odor of a wedding. The remaining wayward girls stay indoors. It continues to rain all day. They are edgy. I huddle over my bowl of soup.

# Chapter 80
## After the 2$^{nd}$ Coming

It is several thousand years later. You have withered for centuries on the coast of Ireland. Your just reward has come.

They open a wall in the sky and pull down the Great Hide-A-Way Bed. It is a dry white terrain of dusty sheets. In the obscure corners you note Childe Roland's footprints. Gnarled vines choke the brass bedposts.

Your clinical lover comes in, her pale flesh perfumed to hide the stench of time. She has the clatter of Roman legions in her belly. Now she shows you where the dinosaurs are buried. She opens the mineral caves of her womb. Your feast awaits.

It was a bad lay. You are dissatisfied with Heaven. Imagine the angels' rage when you tell her so.

## Chapter 81
## The Lonely Fat Man Hides His Shame

One half of the earth is covered in darkness. The Martians landed in 1958. No one knows. They took away our imagination and left us with reason and knowledge. The effects are beginning to show. The only clues to the event are to be found in the comic-book literature of the period. I'm doing a research paper on it for school. I've assembled hundreds of different comic books, all issued in 1958. I bought them from the estate of a dying pop artist.

One half of the world is covered by darkness. It is a seething sea of formless anguish. We sail it with Columbus in his fierce pride. You fall overboard into the slow music. The formless forms engulf you. There is no rescue party.

One half of the earth is covered in darkness. It is only the turning of the globe, they insist. I spend all weekend poring over Bugs Bunny, searching the skies of Daffy Duck for UFOs.

# Chapter 82
## Falfe Profits

The waitress comes over and wipes my table clean. She does not dry it. She missed a spot; she frets over it from across the room. The air blowers are humming. All the potted palms have disappeared.

There is a Band-Aid on the inside of my elbow where they took the blood test. I'm favoring this arm. If the test is positive, I'm to be castrated. If the test is negative, I get to live out the rest of my natural life in Long Beach.

My clinical lover comes to me destroyed, wrapped in shredded, soiled bedsheets. Her face is haggard and grimy in shame. She clutches a plastic bottle of tranquilizers in her hands scarred from the spring factory.

I kiss her forehead and forgive her. The winds continue to howl.

# Chapter 83
## Road

I walk and I walk and I walk and still it is no closer. It is a function of human emotion. The authorities have closed down the Flea Circus. I walk through the night and through the next day, which is dark, past the western walls of the House of Affluence, on a road I am unable to touch.

They make the bed in the dusty corners between the stars. I am glad of something I can feel.

My inventory has rotted into a million crumbled, worded scraps of paper. The spiders and purple-backed crabs crawl out of the walls and drag it away.

# Chapter 84
## The Cube

So now that all is gone, what remains is the hideous face of Death in the corner, mimicking Jesus Christ in the foetal position, and Mary Magdalene, always on the outskirts, pouring balm and salve from a holy vessel into the dirt where it foams white. I invite them to a secluded place in this book for a little get-together, a party of sorts. It is a cubicle of uncertain color, constructed from planks of wood taken from the belly of my clinical lover before the splitting of the atom. It is the corner of a page, bordered on the two open sides by intricate, repetitive fountain-pen designs.

A ragged man comes in from out of the rain, muttering that he is old, that he is not new, and I offer him soup. That is only the beginning; there is tea and honey, and penny buttermilk biscuits in the oven. Mary Magdalene changes into dry clothes. I am reminded of her status. Objective reality has finally and rightfully dissolved, and we are only waiting for this temporary congestion of the soul to pass.

# Chapter 85
## Castilian Sister

Jeremiah, Star-Poet, who resides on top icy blue postcard mountains sent from Madrid, acts as my defense lawyer. Because he has a bushy mustache and we say he looks like a fruit vendor, he is moving to Olvera Street. His Mexican friend with the pickup truck helps. I come along too, to help, and so that we can discuss the case.

This Mexican man is very stern and says nothing. He drives the truck like it was an animal and smokes endless unfiltered cigarettes. He never lights a new one; this endless cigarette is simply always hanging on his lower lip, as long now as it was five minutes ago. You never see him flick an ash. Not wanting to take his eyes off her, he brings his Castilian sister along. She is from Spain and wears long black-lace dresses. Her silky black hair is done up in a bun, and she has a peasant-work fan in it.

She stands to the side as Jeremiah and her brother unload furniture off the truck. I notice that she is smoking so I ask her for a cigarette. She laughs when I light it.

"What's so funny?"

"You are doing it backwards."

"Backwards? What do you mean?"

"You lit the wrong end. That is not how we do it in Madrid. In Madrid we light the filter."

"Doesn't it taste like plastic?"

"Plastic is a very nice thing," she says.

"One half of the earth is in darkness . . ."

"What is that?"

"An old American proverb."

Jeremiah and the Mexican man are trying to keep the pickup from rolling back down the hill as they unload it. The Castilian Sister is commenting in Spanish on how wonderful American sidewalks are. She is pure and innocent as a child and is in love with our sewage systems. She asks me the English word for gutters. Not wanting to anger her brother, I pretend that I don't know.

"However you say it, they are very nice."

"Yes," I agree. She wants me to take her to see some more of our sidewalks and gutters, so we go for a stroll around the block.

When we return we find Jeremiah and the Mexican man in the living room of the new house, arranging the furniture. The brother seems very angry at me. He models a couch out of terra-cotta and says that it only needs one more thing to make it complete.

"Do you have any physical remains?" he asks me.

"What do you mean?" I'm aware that he is very angered. His face is turning red.

"Physical remains! Of your rape and murder! Pubic hairs!"

"You have a morbid sense of humor," I answer.

# Chapter 86
## The 29th Whore

I ran through the House of Affluence, burning each locked room behind me as I left it. The tall flames turned the night sky red. The shriek of the players; the moan of burning horses. Many priceless promptbooks were lost. There is a notice out damning me. I've taken to the streets. The tongues of strangers lash my cheeks. I lose several days in alley visions of Granada.

The 29th whore takes me in under her wing. She has a place with the 28th whore and the Castilian Sister, who left Olvera Street in shame. All night there are footsteps on the stairs. Garbage cans rattle by the windows. We get unexpected bottles of wine by parcel post. They tell lies when police come to the door. I sit reading in the waiting room on a pile of dirty shifts that stink of incense and come. At midnight the last customer leaves and we turn on the TV set. The Castilian Sister rolls a number and I notice for the first time that she has legs like an athlete. I take a hit and another hit by the blue light of King Kong and the 29th whore brings me a beer. She asks how it feels to be a celebrity in Madrid. I'm flying with Lindbergh and there's a fly in my cockpit; I've got a map but the fog is thick; a brown paper bag full of sandwiches. The 29th whore has luxurious brown hair. She's short and started her career as a prostitute only last Wednesday, still smelling of talcum powder. We are undaunted by yet another night of rain. She sings like a canary in the bath tub, saying that she had a year of Spanish in ninth grade. Before I lay her under the water, we discuss Chinese devices, bamboo, and the whites of their eyes turned yellow.

# Chapter 87
## Where's Daddy?

When you are ready, it will fall upon you. With the coming of rain, you remember something about a temple in the trees and the clinical lover, strangled in her white robes, lying by the edge of the pond. There are blue marks on her white throat.

Where did you come from? Somewhere near Los Angeles? Beyond the hills? Are you still in high school? Did you just get out of the army? How many letters has she sent you? Did you go into her room? What exactly does her face look like? What is the precise color of her hair?

Her father digs a pit in the front yard. Evil drives a shovel deep into the soil, slicing roots and scraping against rock at the bottom. I don't know. I don't know. I don't know, but her eyes are bright, stabbing me with their opal fire. I tremble with the cold, and the deathly green of the lawn sympathizes with me.

His hands are red with the soil. They are twisting, clammy hands, fatty like those of a child who tortures insects and small animals. He plunges the steel blade into the earth. Sweat is unfamiliar on his brow and he clenches the shovel with desperate white knuckles. Over and over he fucks her with his eyes. I grab the shovel and lunge at his face. The side of his head caves in. I blind those eyes. I dig out his charcoal bowels with my hands; nothing but dry ash. I bury him under the lawn.

We go into her kitchen for lunch, I'm trembling and the blood drips off my fingers into the coffee. My clinical lover is at the stove with her back to me. She is making soup. I want to put my hands around her waist under the apron, but her mother is watching us from her ladder in the living room where she is cleaning the crystal chandelier. Her dirty rag goes into the bucket of soapy water and then up to the crystal, where a rivulet runs down her arm. She glares at me as she climbs down from her ladder. "Where's Daddy?" she asks. My clinical lover does not answer.

The mother goes out front to turn on the sprinklers and her husband's blood rains over the city of Goleta. It sprinkles the station wagons and drips from the high tension lines. It runs in little rivers down the front window of the real-estate office.

A shriek is frozen between two mountains. Under the stars I hitch a ride back to the hotel.

# Chapter 88
## Pepper Shaker

I walk and I walk and I walk, picking names out of the black mass of broken mussel shells and woven seaweed vines that lie along the beach, names like the droning hum of electric fans in the air-conditioned cafeteria.

The woman has just cleaned off my table, but not wiped it dry, and there is a haphazard wash of soapy water across the smooth Formica top. It is thin and quickly dries into a dull whitish film. I smear its trail with my thumb, changing by 90° the grain of its reflection.

In the chrome top of the pepper shaker the entire room is mirrored. It is a minute, perfect image, like you would find in a canvas by a Flemish old master. I am a very large shadow, filling most of the chrome surface, and above me the fluorescent lights wrap around the circle of holes that pepper is shaken through. My table fills the bottom of the cap, rippling over the screw-on threads. To the left of my shadow are the other tables in the cafeteria, and above them, the narrow light of the windows, a bluish light compared to the yellow of the overhead lamps. In this narrow rectangle of blue window light, two foreshortened buildings rise gray-pink. There is a small gap between the buildings through which a hill, the steep grade of the northbound freeway, can be seen. Squat cars slowly climb the hill. The heated air makes them shimmer and glisten in the setting sun. When they reach the top of the hill, they fall off into space. Past the hill it is cool; the world is in a blue-green twilight. A slight wind off the ocean soon turns the air cold. Children are running home down asphalt streets and a clock is ticking. Names are being spoken as the final rays of the sun touch the highest and farthest street where my clinical lover rolls a hoop along the crest. And through the hoop's circle, the red surf and the deep, deep green of the sea.

Beyond the sea the dark mass rises, confused like a primeval vegetable. It is speaking the names. It sounds like mechanical movements inside my chest.

# Chapter 89
## Moorifh Apes

I took an axe to the knickknack mantel. I ravished nightgowns hanging in the closet. The cross took root and grew, nourished by my blood. No one came to mass; the church is empty. I bled in my soup. You have wings and I worship you. There you are! Over the housetops! You are lying like an exhausted casserole in the oven. The pressure cooker has consumed your brains. They are dishing them out in the seminary.

I can't get the hash lit. It looks like leaden crystals of galena in the bowl of my pipe. My typewriter has disappeared into the fog. It flounders, limp as tapioca pudding. The true poet has severed his vocal cords; he has filed suit against the dictionary. Wisdom was exiled, Eros has gone into hiding. I'm sitting here in the cafeteria, crying.

You have wings and I follow you. You lose me in the fog. I am found hysterical and soothed by Moorish apes.

# Chapter 90
## The 28th Whore

The 28th whore leads me upstairs to her room. She takes off her neck brace and begins filling the bath; it is an old porcelain tub, with brass spigots corroded green. The walls of the bathroom are mottled green, with strips of old red velvet wallpaper that flake off like sunburnt skin. Carte de visite photographs of young men in top hats are randomly Scotch-taped to the walls. The room is filling up with steam from the hot water. She slips out of her dress and peels off her panties. Her skin is amazing in that it is uniformly tan all over, without the usual few patches of white. We get in and thrash around awhile to get accustomed to the scalding water. We're up to our throats in bubble-bath suds. She reaches over and pulls a bottle of Scotch out from behind the toilet.

"*Una taza, por favor*," she says, pointing to a Dixie cup dispenser by the sink.

"Just a dirty trick to get me to stand up," I mutter, tiptoeing across the black and white checkerboard tiles.

"*Qué?*"

"*Nada*. Here." I hand her the cups.

"*Gracias*." She fills them to the brim and hands me one.

"Thank you. I once wrote a paper on Emily Dickinson's 'I taste a liquor never brewed' . . . and so on, about how the booze could be pearly because the alcohol floats on the top and refracts the light, but I suppose you wouldn't know about that."

"*Qué?*"

"I said I love your tits, they're beautiful."

"*Qué?*"

I reach over and feel both of them under the suds.

"Oh! *Gracias.*"

"No trouble at all."

"Pop!" she says, sticking her finger into a bubble.

"Right. I like the way they make dents in the foam. Like two icebreakers plowing through the sudsy arctic."

She laughs like a Brazilian bird and pours the cup of Scotch over her breasts and stomach. She puts her arms around my neck and pulls me down with her under the water.

CR

After making love we lay in her bed of seaweed, listening to Dick Whittinghill on the radio talking about his cat. In our thoughts it had become summer. The lawns had just been cut and the air smelled of wet grass. We walked through it barefoot and it made the soles of our feet green. I stepped on a snail. Summer ended. I buried her corpse in a shallow grave behind the Flea Circus.

# Chapter 91
## The Witch of Atlas & the Dark Mafs
## at the End of the Beach

The Witch of Atlas lifted large books of maps onto the table. The Thing took up stamp collecting. Together they hung around the Goleta Post Office on balmy summer afternoons, badgering the bald-headed postal clerks. The tips of the Thing's fingers began to get very gummy from stamps. It washed its hands in the drinking fountain at the park. All to no avail. Dogs on walks knew well its error. Concrete was its enemy. It took out vengeance on fire hydrants. Autumn was coming and there was no way out. It turned to the *I Ching* to learn its fate. The *I* said that the Thing's "vessel has been overturned to empty it of rotting meat." That seemed true enough. It hovered over the land. Its poverty became yours. Together you and It reached an agreement with the ocean. The terms were severe, but at last there was an end in sight to your troubles. It praised all savage plants. It walked the beach in newfound glory. This was a good myth. It watched the myth for hours on the television. It didn't mind reruns of that sort.

## Chapter 92
## Before *The Trial*


I am sitting in the lobby of the Goleta Hotel, reliving the highlights of the year 1959. They have just changed the back of the penny from two bronze wheat stalks to a picture of the Lincoln Memorial Hotel and Convention Center of Greater Downtown Goleta. This saddens me greatly. Grain litters the floor around the TV set. The 27 remaining whores are planted in a row before it. On comes a film classic from yesteryear, *The Trial.*

# Chapter 93
## *The Trial*, A Film Claffic from Yefteryear

Narrator: "The west wing of the House of Affluence has been locked off since the end of the last century. It is the closet primeval, extending its wide cell over the seas and deep into tropical antiquity. . . ."

Barker: "I came to be one dark and stormy Goleta evening at the Flea Circus on upper Crux. It was a most singular building, quite large, an old warehouse made up to look like a movie theatre. It was very late, and as there was no one around, I ventured to jimmy open one of the side doors. I had been consumed by a morbid curiosity concerning the Flea Circus ever since my arrival, two weeks prior, in the fair city of Goleta. I wanted desperately to see the famous Black Beast said to be housed there. Newspaper accounts of the creature had filled me with awe and terror, and I had vowed solemnly to myself to see it. The police had closed down the spectacle with no reasons given, but I was determined to have just one glimpse of it if it was the last thing I did. I opened the door and entered the dark building, and this is the tale of what I experienced. . . ."

# Chapter 94
## To the Tower

Three insurance salesmen and I are traveling by car through the rainforest. There is a terrible storm going on and we are forced off the road into a mud ditch. The nearest town is eight miles back.

"It's going to be a bad night."

"I'll say."

"Bad bit of luck, this."

"Most trying."

We are walking along the roadside, hoping that a motorist will come along to assist us. There is a flash of lightning, and through the dense treetops I catch a glimpse of a tower to the north. We leave the road and head towards it. The undergrowth is very thick and we can hardly see farther than five feet in any direction. We keep talking back and forth so as not to lose any member of our company. The heavily thorned bushes tear at my clothes and lash my face with cuts. My limbs are half frozen in the icy downpour and I am continually being tripped by the snake-like vines that weave through the roots and spongy humus of the forest floor. In spite of my boots, the mud leeches are already attaching their sucking-mouthed bodies to my legs. We are unsure of the way. The Allstate man had a compass but he lost it in the mud when tripped by a vine, so we are guided now by sheer intuition. I say to the left more, but the others insist that the tower is straight ahead. There is another flash of lightning.

"I saw it!" cries the Prudential man, pointing to the far right and looking as if he had seen a ghost. "I saw the tower! Over there!"

"Are you sure?" we ask, having seen nothing.

"I would stake my life on it."

"He's daft," the Lloyds of London man says.

"No, I swear! I saw it!"

The Prudential man, the Allstate man, and I agree to turn to the right. "Are you coming?" we call back to the Lloyd's of London man.

"Humph," he grumbles, following us.

I am taking the lead now. The vines have become thicker and our way is impossibly slow. Through some great piece of fortune I stumble over an old, corroded brass pipe.

"Eureka!" I cry back to the others.

"What is it?"

"What in the Devil's name?"

"An old brass pipe!"

"And of what use is that piece of junk to us?" calls out the Lloyd's of London man.

"All the use in the world! I'll use it as a machete, to hack away the vines and undergrowth from our path."

"The path is clear enough," he retorts.

I hack left and right at the thick green wall before us and our progress improves. My arm soon tires but there is no stopping now. After what seems like hours we enter a clearing, and the tower, on top of the west wing of an old house, comes into full view.

The men send up a heartfelt cheer, all except for the Lloyd's of London man who strokes his full beard with his bleeding fingers and snorts, "And what, if I may ask, in the Devil is it, now that we've found it?"

"Our salvation!"

"Humph. How are you so sure that anyone even lives here anymore?"

"What matter? It offers shelter—"

But my words are cut off when the door of the house opens and in the doorway appears a man with a lantern and a shotgun.

## Chapter 95
### A Slight Pause for This Commercial Meſſage

Large man in light blue suit sitting behind desk: "Friends, buy land in beautiful Goleta. You can have lakeside acreage for no money down. Enjoy fishing . . . nature hikes . . . fun in the sun. We build the A-frame, you finish the inside as a family project. No money down, small monthly payments. Send now for maps . . . brochures . . . Free . . . everything is free . . . no obligation. Call Richmond 999-9999999999999999999999999."

# Chapter 96
## And Now We Return to This Afternoon's Feature Film

Once inside we explained our situation, and the man, who identified himself as a retired Air Force pilot, laid the gun down against the side of his chair and bid us to sit by the fire which his servant had been building. The servant, whom I recognized as the Manikin from the Flea Circus, much aged and the worse so for typhoid fever, brought us each a cup of hot broth and then announced that he was retiring for the night.

"And what brings you gentlemen to the rainforest?" the pilot asked.

"Investigation of an insurance claim. Filed by the Great Dirt Ship Company against the Ocean Company. More than that we are not at liberty to disclose," answered the Allstate man.

"Confidentiality of evidence and all that rubbish."

"And sir," added the Lloyd's of London man with a sneer, "what brings you to live in this god-awful bloody hole of a jungle?"

Thinking this a rude question, I cut it off by saying, "Thank our lucky stars we saw your tower! It was a heaven-send."

The pilot gasped, his whole personage gripped with unspeakable terror. We rushed towards him to insure that he still breathed, but he shoved us away and leapt to his feet, pointing his finger at me and saying in a weak, vicious voice, "Mr. Barker! I pronounce you guilty! You have brought them all to die by the deeds of your own hands and organs. Under no circumstances are you to mention the tower again! That goes for all of you; stay away from the entire west wing if you value your lives. Your rooms are at the top of the stairs, to the left. I will deal with you in the morning, Mr. Barker. Good evening, gentlemen."

# Chapter 97
## What Hath Sir Richard Wrought?

We found our separate rooms and said good night, almost afraid to speak. The only illumination in the room was provided by a small gas lamp that stood on top of an old walnut roll-top desk in the corner. I sat on the canopied double bed in the opposite corner, watching the flickering lamp send animated shades across the walls and ceiling. Despite near exhaustion from our jungle experience prior to coming here, I was unable to sleep, so shaken and puzzled was I by the strange incident that had just taken place downstairs by the fireside. I was unable to make a logical connection between the forbidden tower and any fault that the pilot might find with me personally. Yet just the mentioning of the tower had seemed to bring on the attack of rage that resulted in my condemnation. And there was something strangely familiar about the pilot himself. Then suddenly it dawned on me; the so-called retired Air Force pilot was none other than Sir Richard Wrought! Well disguised, but nonetheless his very self!

I had been sitting there in a stiff position, staring blankly at the lamp and going over these events in my mind for about a quarter of an hour, when I heard footsteps in the hall outside my door. I jumped with fright, accidentally knocking over a vase of Venus fly-traps from the nightstand that went crashing to the floor. The steps stopped dead in their tracks. I froze so as not to make a sound, and my eyes fixed themselves on the door. For nearly five minutes this silent contest of nerves dragged on and then I heard a metallic click of a key in the lock.

"Who goes there?" My voice tried to be a courageous one, but failed.

There was no answer, only retreating footsteps

down the hall. I got up and tried the door. It was locked. I had been uneasy, even frightened, before, but now I had a very real terror for my safety. I ran to the window, but when I ripped the heavy velvet curtains aside, I met with cold, ungiving iron bars. I was trapped in this room. I stood, feeling very melancholy, staring out through the bars into the rainy night, when I thought I could make out a dark shadow against the sky. It was the forbidden tower. Lightning once again lit the sky, and for an instant I could very clearly see the crumbling stones of the tower rising above the west wing, the large window of an unlit cell near the tower's top, and a tall unhuman figure in a large blue suit staring out with fierce eyes from the window. I was overcome with an almost religious horror: the Thing! It appeared to have been watching me, and I had seen It for a fraction of a second, but now the tower was shrouded in darkness. It must have been attracted by the light from my room when I pulled the curtains aside. Was It still watching me? I panicked and immediately pulled the curtains shut again, but the fabric was weak with age and dry rot, and they tore right off the rods.

"Jesus!"

It was still watching me. There was nothing else to do except drag the bed over to the window and prop it up to block off the Monster's view of me. My heart was pounding and the adrenaline thick in my veins, so that I lifted the bed, which weighed at least a half-ton, with ease and slammed it up against the window.

"Christ!" bellowed the Lloyd's of London man from across the hall. "Keep it down in there! A body can't sleep!"

"Sorry," I called back. "Nightmare." I suppose I could have simply put out the lamp instead; that would have concealed me from the Monster's eyes, but I was determined to find a way out of the room, and darkness would have hampered me greatly.

# Chapter 98
## Salvage

With the bed up against the window it was certain that I wouldn't get to sleep tonight. I went over to the roll-top desk and opened it. The thing was jammed with old yellowing papers, which I inspected and found to be mostly antiquated insurance policies. They were the oldest forms of this sort I had ever run across, being written by hand with a broad pen on leathery old paper. They were decorated with red wax seals and tax stamps that bore a picture of an upright lion with clawing paws printed in feeble black ink. Thinking that it might be possible to draw a claim on some of these century-and-a-half-old policies, I stuffed a few down my shirtfront. Perhaps the beneficiaries had never collected; it was worth investigating. The rest of the policies I shoved onto the floor to make room for my further explorations into the desk.

This act uncovered a row of cubbyholes at the back of the desk, stuffed with curious old odds and ends. One was full of nothing but prehistoric bobby pins and medieval rubber bands. They were useless but historically delightful, so I put a few of each into my shirt pocket. (The reader might think it foolish of me to trifle with these bizarre objects while danger was closing in from all quarters, but I can only defend my actions by appealing to the reader's sense of intuition and assuring him that the instinct which had so far succeeded in guiding me through life now led me to believe that the escape from this room was surely to be found in the desk. If you don't like it, assume that I was rescued by IRS agents in disguise as door-to-door orangutans in drag.) In the next cubbyhole, which was stained by the ancient spillage of an ink bottle, I found a stuffed sea gull. The ink was smeared on its dusty white feathers and the claws and beak had turned brittle and leathery like a second-hand alligator-skin couch. I felt the reassuring presence of Max Ernst and the whole troupe of early 20th century Dadaists. But the thing smelled terribly.

In the next cubbyhole was nothing but a small pearlescent button off of a woman's dress. Close examination told me that it had been the one that fastens exactly midway between two full, lovely breasts and maintains decency. This, together with the bobby pins, led me to believe that a young lady was present somewhere in the house; the west wing I feared. I was starting to get an erection in anticipation, but these fond thoughts were quickly arrested by the discovery of a December issue of the *Reader's Disgust* in the next cubbyhole. I pulled myself together as I put the little button, made sweaty in the palm of my hand, into the pocket of my jeans. I picked up two books which I had found with the *Disgust*, and was turning to the title page of the first, when I heard a ghastly sound from down the hallway: a quiet, sickening sound like a greasy fried hot dog being squeezed to a pulp in a strong fist. My stomach turned over and I fixed my eyes in terror on the door. The sound subsided, but the only way to quiet my nerves and alleviate my frustration at finding that god-awful periodical was to treat myself to a smoke.

I looked at my watch; it was 2:31 in the morning, August 19th, 1742. I lit my pipe and sat musing upon the Surgeon General's report. I kept my eyes on the door. It rippled and moved with the fluctuations of the gas lamp, but did not open. I was locked in, but then again, I was safer with the door locked than with it open. The problem was whether I would open it getting out or they would open it getting in. Quite a philosophical puzzle, but of course my pipe always puts me in a philosophical frame of mind. Soon I drew ash and realized that my smoke was over.

I opened the first book to its title page. It was a study on whether or not Shelley masturbated, put out by the Scholar's Press. There was an interesting account on page 91 about Mary Shelley's capacity for orgasm, but the *Reader's Disgust* glared disapprovingly at me. I threw both books in the corner with anger and opened the third book. It looked familiar. It was called *inventory* and there were an endless number of pages. It smelled of the ocean and there were particles of sand in between the pages. Looking it over, I discovered that it was boring rubbish. Next I went to the desk drawers. The top one held a sleeping cat, very well fed, and purring with loud content.

"Shut up that bloody noise!" the Lloyd's of London man shouted from across the hall. I quickly closed the drawer.

"Sorry, asthma . . ."

"Humph," he snorted.

"Irritable fellow," I mumbled.

"I heard that!"

"Sorry."

The middle drawer was full of Spanish gold coins with Franco's face on them and also a mimeographed pamphlet called *The 101 Positions of Fucking* with crudely drawn illustrations. I bit into one of the coins; it's a lead counterfeit, I thought at first, but eventually it softened in my hand and I realized that it was a cheap waxy chocolate covered with gold foil. I put some of these into my handkerchief and tied a bundle which I fastened to my belt to stave off any possible future hunger.

I began to hear sounds in the hall again. There were two pairs of feet walking, or rather tiptoeing, at different speeds. One was very slow and clumsy. This I decided must be the Manikin, old and diseased. The second was fast and sprightly, the agile old "pilot," Sir Richard Wrought. They were closing in for the kill.

I pulled open the bottom drawer, which was much larger than the other drawers. It was filled with glass eyeballs. I shoveled these out and they went bouncing like marbles around the floor. It made a terrible racket and I could hear voices in the hall and the fitting of a key into the lock. I shoveled faster. At the bottom was a brass ring. I gave it a tug and the bottom of the drawer came out, revealing a dark stairway going down into the pitch blackness of a subterranean shaft. I crawled into the drawer and descended the steps until only my head was still in the drawer. Then I pulled the drawer shut with my teeth, except for a crack through which to spy. And just in time, for the door burst open and the Manikin and Sir Richard Wrought entered the room with bloody hands and a meat cleaver.

# Chapter 99
## D. Alighieri

"What in God's name?" gasped Sir Richard Wrought, alias the Air Force pilot, as he looked around the room and saw the broken flowerpot lying in pieces in a mound of soil on the floor, the bed leaning up against the window, the torn drapes hanging by a thread from the bent curtain rod, and a thousand glass eyeballs bouncing and rolling around the room which was littered with old insurance policies and the scattered pages of the *Reader's Disgust*.

"Holy shit," said the Manikin.

I stood in total blackness except for the crack of the drawer through which I watched them as they paced the floor, ranting and raving and wondering to where I had disappeared. They were definitely surprised to find me gone, and the pilot was unable to conceal his utter disappointment at not having the opportunity to use his weapons upon me. By the direction in which the stairs descended, I realized that this shaft must be a secret entrance into the west wing, and I was both frightened and fascinated at the prospect of visiting the forbidden rooms. The pilot, Sir Richard, seemed at a loss of what to do next. He had been prepared for the execution, and I had to feel sorry for him. It suddenly occurred to me why the Lloyd's of London man was not complaining about the noise anymore; there was fresh, thick blood on the Manikin's butcher knife. I made a silent sign of the cross.

"Darling!" Sir Richard bellowed. In walked Mrs. Ghast in a maid's uniform. Sir Richard whispered something in her ear and then gave her a little pinch on the ass.

"Yes, sir; right away, sir." She shuffled off, blushing.

Sir Richard and the Manikin began ransacking the room. They walked over to the desk and I shut the drawer just in time.

I could see nothing. My feet felt their way down. I counted twenty steps and it began to get colder. The steps felt damp under my worn-soled shoes and I almost slipped. I heard something and stopped. It was the sound of running water. I touched the wall and it was wet. Fearing that the Manikin and Sir Richard might see me if they should happen to open the desk drawer, I descended even deeper into the black. I was terrified to think what lay ahead of me in the dark, but the thought of their bloodied weapons drove me deeper. At fifty steps down I could no longer hear the noise above made by their rummaging through the desk for me. At sixty-three steps down I heard Sir Richard's voice, very far away, swearing foully. I looked over my shoulder and saw a tiny square of light way above me with Sir Richard's face stuck in it.

"Come on back up here, you dirty little son of a bitch!" he called.

I raced downward, stumbling and falling in the pitch black on the slippery steps, and hit my head against the wall when I stopped. Sitting in a painful huddle on the steps with my head in my hands, I waited for at least five minutes in surrender until I realized that Sir Richard wasn't coming down after me.

"Come on up, you little son of a bitch," the wee voice continued to call down to me.

"Suck off!"

"You little pervert turd! You shall be brought to justice!"

"Eat shit!"

"Who will pay? Who do you think is willing to accept the blame? Who will pay for this?"

"Your old lady wears army boots." I saw the small pink circle that was his face turn red, and then the light disappeared. I sat there wondering what would become of me and if my escape was permanent or temporary. I lit a match and looked at my watch; it was 3:15, sometime in September, 1833. With what little light the match gave off I looked around me. The reason for the dampness became apparent; coming out of the wall every few feet like lanterns were corroded bronze spigots that continually dripped water down the wall and onto the steps. They were green with decomposition and under each was a slimy fan of mold caused by the stones being constantly wet. I held the match closer to the wall and noticed to my amazement that there were some names and dates carved into the stone. Some had been obliterated by the eternal flowing of the water over them, wearing the stone away. My match was burning close to my fingers and getting too hot to hold, but just before I dropped it onto the steps with a hiss, I read one of the carved names:

"D. Alighieri—1305"

# Chapter 100
## Tools

I continued down the steps, making my way in the dark for what I guessed to be half an hour. I could have lit another match to see my way and keep from stumbling, but I only had one more left and felt that I must keep it for an emergency. Suddenly the steps ended and I felt cobblestone beneath my feet. I walked forwards a ways, but the tunnel was apparently curved and I had to feel my way along the wall. There was a feeble light ahead that grew stronger and when I rounded a sharp corner, I saw a long straight tunnel ahead of me, lit by drooling old tapers every few hundred feet. It was a relief to have light again.

I pulled one of the candles out of its wrought-iron holder on the wall and carried it with me. It was much faster going with the light, although it revealed such grotesque gothic forms carved into the vaults and coffers of the tunnel that I was more afraid with it than without: icons and images of Anglo-Saxon saints, and devilish stone gnomes and mortar gargoyles draped in cobwebs and staring at me with dead Mediterranean eyes. In some of the vaults stood ivory altars stained brown with old blood and the shriveled gum of dried animal remains, and in others, piles of human bones adorned with encrusted, tarnished jewels and thinly beaten gold breastplates. The tunnel was thick with moist dust and silent except for the sound of my shoes on the wet stones.

Then I entered a vast, dismal chamber and saw something which stopped me dead in my tracks: there were rows upon rows, neatly piled, of thousands of immaculately new tools. Innumerable in size and type: wrenches, screwdrivers, files, saws, hammers, pliers—all quietly glistening with an awe-inspiring peace that spoke of the beginning of time. I stood for a very long time in a deep rapture, hypnotized by the chrome-steel glisten and sparkling of millions of stellar tools set in brilliant vaulted clusters light-years from my greedy hands.

Tools!

I was drunk with power!

I rushed forwards to the vault where the wrenches were stacked to the ceiling, afraid to reach out and touch them. I felt a driving warmth inside my loins and tears streamed from my eyes as I dragged my sweaty finger across the smooth steel and delighted in its ancient coldness. I could feel the heat of the antediluvian forges, trapped forever within the crystalline cells of chrome, zinc, and cold-rolled steel. I ran from vault to vault, taking one of each type tool until my pockets were overflowing and my coat weighed almost as much as I did. Then I picked up my candle and walked on, feeling only the goodness of the tools weighing me down as I dragged along.

# Chapter 101
## Sweet Young Faces

Nothing but darkness day and night. I continue to walk. The cities are in ruin. Only the churches stand; the feeble yellow light from their windows pours out over the land like storm warnings into the dark.

One by one, I find the bodies on the shore. They have such sweet young faces.

*About the Author*

David Barker is a poet and short-story writer whose work has appeared in dozens of chapbooks, little magazines, and literary anthologies in the U. S. and Europe. David lives with his wife in western Oregon and works as a research analyst. They have four daughters and two grandsons.

# *Colophon*

*Death at the Flea Circus* was published in May 2011. Designed and typeset by Bill Roberts in Dover, Delaware. The cover was designed by Ray Nichols at Lead Graffiti and printed via letterpress on a Vandercook Universal III. The cover & title page was digitally set in Wyld and Blackadder ITC. The text was digitally set in Wyld, with accents in My Underwood, AR Christy, Isabella, Times New Roman & American Typewriter.

Limited to an edition of 260 copies;

200 copies perfect bound in wraps with dust jacket which is printed letterpress on Canson Mi-Teintes 98 lb (160 gsm) paper.

50 signed hardcover copies, numbered 1-50. Quarter bound in 180 year old repurposed sheep vellum & printed letterpress on Canson Mi-Teintes 98 lb (160 gsm) paper.

10 signed deluxe copies in oversized custom clamshell with drawers and lettered A-J. Contains a hard cover and a paperback book, both signed, as well as appropriate inclusions stored in the clamshell drawers.